SPARK

A HENRY HOLT MYSTERY

A HENRY HOLT MYSTERY

SPARK

JOHN LUTZ

HENRY HOLT AND COMPANY
NEW YORK

Henry Holt and Company, Inc.
Publishers since 1866
115 West 18th Street
New York, New York 10011

Henry Holt® is a registered trademark
of Henry Holt and Company, Inc.

Published in Canada by Fitzhenry & Whiteside Limited,
91 Granton Drive, Richmond Hill, Ontario L4B 2N5.

Library of Congress Cataloging-in-Publication Data
Lutz, John.
Spark / John Lutz.—1st ed.
p.   cm.—(A Henry Holt mystery)
I. Title.
PS3562.U854S67   1993   92-25182
813′.54—dc20   CIP

ISBN 0-8050-1993-6 (acid-free paper)

First Edition—1993

DESIGNED BY LUCY ALBANESE

Printed in the United States of America
All first editions are printed
on acid-free paper.∞

1   3   5   7   9   10   8   6   4   2

FOR JO ANN HAUN

Only stay quiet, while my mind remembers
The beauty of fire from the beauty of embers.

—JOHN MASEFIELD,
On Growing Old

SPARK

A HENRY HOLT MYSTERY

1

"WHAT ARE you, in your mid-forties?"

"That's what I am," Carver said, staring at Hattie Evans, wondering if "Hattie" was a nickname. She was wearing quite a hat, a prim and proper red mushroomlike thing with a truncated little stem on top. It was ninety degrees outside and she was wearing a hat. He had to admit, despite her sixty-plus years it made her look jaunty.

"Well, you listen, Mr. Carver, I don't play games and I won't be brushed aside."

"Didn't intend either of those things," Carver said. He tried a smile. He was a fierce-looking man but he knew his smile was unexpectedly beautiful and disarming. Used it often. Hattie seemed unimpressed.

As she'd entered Carver's office on Magellan and sat down before his desk, he'd seen her faded but quick blue eyes flit to where his cane leaned, but she didn't ask about it. She sat poised with military rigidity in the chair and pressed her knees tightly together beneath the skirt of her navy-blue dress. It was an expensive dress but old and a little threadbare, as was her once-stylish—possibly—hat. She was a whipcord-lean woman, not tall, and she had the look about her of someone who'd endured a lot but was ready for more. Though she'd never been pretty, crow's feet at the corners of her eyes, pain and experience etched like wounds at the corners of her lips, gave her narrow, alert face a kind of character that held the eye.

"I'm sixty-seven years old," she said, "in case you're wondering. In case you've got ideas."

"Ideas?"

"You know what I'm talking about. Those kinds of ideas. Don't pretend you're slow. I took the time and trouble to find out about you before I came here."

Carver sighed. "I don't have those kinds of ideas, Hattie. Anyway, I can see you're not the sort to try them on." He shot her his smile again. "Not that some men wouldn't like to." Such charm. Was it working?

She glared at him.

"You mentioned Lieutenant Desoto sent you," Carver prompted, noticing for the first time that Hattie Evans smelled not unpleasantly like roses. Desoto was Carver's longtime friend on the Orlando Police Department. The friend who'd urged him not to surrender, to go into private investigation after a holdup man—a kid, really—had shattered Carver's kneecap with a bullet and left his leg bent at a thirty-degree angle for life.

"The lieutenant said the police couldn't really delve into my case because I didn't have enough evidence. Have you ever heard of such a thing?"

"All the time," Carver said. He leaned back in his chair and extended his stiff left leg out beneath the desk, digging his moccasin heel into the carpet.

"He told me he had a hunch, though, that I wasn't just talking through my hat, so he recommended I come to you. Was he right to do that?"

"Talk and we'll decide," Carver told her.

"My husband, Jerome, and I live—at least I live—out in Solartown. Do you know where that is?"

Carver nodded. Solartown was a sprawling retirement community east of Orlando, hundreds of almost identical houses all built within the past ten years. It was one of those self-contained middle-class retirement communities like Sun City out in Arizona, with its own shops, medical facilities, recreation center. A retiree didn't have to leave the place for any reason other than variety. It was all there: golf, tennis, bingo, swimming, crafts classes, everything but a mortuary.

"Two weeks ago, while we were having watercress sandwiches for lunch, Jerome keeled over dead from a heart attack." Her facial muscles remained immobile as she said that, but glimmers of sorrow passed through her direct blue eyes like windswept clouds. Passed quickly. She wasn't one to wallow in grief.

"I'm sorry," Carver told her.

"Thank you. Jerome and I moved down here to Florida two years ago from St. Louis, after he retired from his job at the brewery. He had a complete medical checkup then and his heart was strong. That city's got the best medical doctors in the world. They wouldn't be mistaken. And his heart was sound when he had his regular checkup two months ago."

"How old was Jerome?"

"Seventy last December third. And in fine shape but for a slightly swollen prostate. We also know his family tree, and heart attacks aren't in his heredity." She stared hard at Carver, as if he should have assimilated what she'd said and drawn a conclusion.

"You aren't convinced he died of a heart attack?" he asked, remembering Desoto had referred her to him. Desoto didn't send him prospective clients lightly.

"I suppose he did," Hattie said, "if that's what the Solartown

Medical Center doctors say was the cause of death. But the question is, why? How?"

"As I understand it," Carver said, "at Jerome's age, it might simply have happened."

"Nothing in this world simply happens, Mr. Carver, despite what the bumper stickers say. I think the note proves that."

"Note?"

"Two days ago I found it in my mailbox, but without a stamp. It was printed in black ink and it said my husband was murdered. It was unsigned, of course. When I went to the police, they seemed to regard the letter as a sadistic practical joke. A young officer patted my shoulder as if I were his pet dog and told me I'd be shocked at what some people could do. I told him nothing shocked me, but he just patted me again. It was only your Lieutenant Desoto who took me at all seriously. He suggested I bring the note, and my story, to you." She crossed her legs, somehow without having separated them. "And here I am."

"Did you bring the note?"

"Of course I did." Her tone of voice made Carver feel momentarily guilty for asking such an obvious question. She drew a white envelope from her blue straw purse and handed it to him. It smelled strongly of roses.

The envelope had her name printed on it in black felt-tip pen. The note inside read simply: "Jerome was murdered. Don't ever think otherwise." The simple, almost childish printing was the same as on the envelope.

He replaced the note in the envelope and laid it on the desk. He said, "The police could be right. It might well be a sadistic prank."

"If you were me, young man, wouldn't you feel compelled to make sure?"

He looked across the desk at her and she gazed back without blinking, a wisp of a woman, all spirit against the storm.

"I can afford to pay you," she assured him. "Jerome was overinsured."

"An investigation might come to nothing."

"That's not exactly a winning attitude, Mr. Carver, but I assure you I comprehend the odds."

Carver had just finished tracking down the missing daughter of a jailed drug dealer. He had nothing else going at the moment. He got a contract from a desk drawer and explained the terms to Hattie. She signed it and then wrote him a retainer check that smelled like roses.

Then she stood up and smiled for the first time. It was a satisfied, inward kind of smile, but it made Carver like her. She was tough and precise and not hobbled by sentiment. If she'd bent at all in her life, it hadn't been one time or one degree more than was necessary.

He laid the contract on top of the crude note. He'd start a file when Hattie left.

Standing very erect, she primly smoothed her skirt down over her bony hips. It had a lot of wool in it for Florida. "Good day, Mr. Carver. I'll expect regular concise reports."

"Were you ever a schoolteacher?"

"Long, long ago. Why do you ask?"

"You remind me of my fourth-grade teacher."

"And you remind me of a rambunctious, obsessive trouble-maker I used to keep after class more often than not to clean blackboard erasers. Reminded me of him the moment I walked in here. That's when I knew I wanted to hire you."

She strode out, the scent of roses in her wake.

He was relieved he hadn't been sent to the principal's office.

2

THE WIND off the ocean pushed in through the cottage window, cool on Carver's bare back that was still wet from his shower. He pulled several pairs of Jockey shorts from his dresser drawer and tossed them on the bed, then levered himself down on the mattress with his cane and wrestled into a pair. Leaned on the cane and stood up.

He caught a glimpse of himself in the big mirror above the dresser, lame but with a lean and muscular upper body, baldheaded except for a fringe of thick curly gray hair above his ears and down the back of his neck. Blue eyes tilted up at the outer corners like a cat's. Sunburned and with a scar at the right corner of his mouth that lent him a cruel expression. A plastic surgeon had once told him the expression could be altered to one more amiable, but Carver had smiled and said no thanks, his looks were an occupational advantage when trying to collect bad debts. His left ear with its missing lobe, the result of a run-in with a knife-wielding madman, could also be made to look better, the surgeon had assured Carver. He'd thought that one over, then decided the hell with it. His looks were the map of his past, and what was anyone without the sum of his experience?

In the mirror, he saw Beth walk into the bedroom. She was a tall and beautiful black woman who looked as cool as light chocolate ice cream in yellow shorts and sleeveless top, her straightened hair combed back off her wide forehead. The shorts were of a modest-enough cut, but her legs still looked impossibly long.

She smiled and said, "You admiring yourself, Fred?"

"Admiring you."

"While you happen to be standing nearly naked in front of the mirror, huh?"

"I was sorta taking stock," he told her, turning away from his reflection.

"Some parts of you are still worthwhile," she said, then glanced at the underwear on the bed, his scuffed leather suitcase that he'd dragged down from the closet shelf. "Travelin' time?"

He'd driven to his Del Moray beach cottage to pack immediately after talking with Hattie Evans. "Just into Orlando," he said. "I figure it'd be best if I stayed at a motel there until I got something cleared up."

He told her about the Hattie Evans case while he got slacks, socks, and his shaving kit and placed them on the bed next to the underwear.

"Sounds as if there might be something in it for *Burrow*," she said, when he'd finished. She was working as a free-lance journalist, mostly for *Burrow*, a small Del Moray paper that specialized in stories the larger and more conservative *Del Moray Chronicle-Bugle* and other Florida papers couldn't or wouldn't touch. She did more conventional reporting, too, and had published several features in both the *Chronicle-Bugle* and the *Orlando Sentinel*. She was no longer taken lightly as a journalist.

"I'll let you know how it's shaping up," Carver said. "I might need your help."

They'd come to a comfortable arrangement whereby they used each other's resources in their work. Beth had contacts in Florida's drug world. She was the widow of drug lord Roberto Gomez and still had reason to fear survivors of his organization. But she'd figured the safest play was for her to go as public as possible instead of hiding, become a journalist whose murder would draw wide media attention. So far it had worked. She'd stayed alive. It didn't hurt, either, that she and Carver were lovers. Carver had a reputation.

"I get my best stories from you, Fred," she said, hip-swaying over and touching his bare shoulder. He felt himself tighten at her touch, wanted to hold her, take her down onto the bed. Not the time for that, he told himself.

"I better finish packing," he said, maybe a bit too crisply.

"I don't muck around in your cases unless you ask," she reminded him.

He hoisted the suitcase onto the bed and let it fall open. "When I do ask," he said, "you're there. I appreciate it. I've come to count on you." The wind gusted in again, pressing her yellow blouse to her lean torso. "What've you got going now?" he asked.

"Doing a piece on police brutality for *Burrow*. Got it about wrapped up."

"Brutality where?"

"Here in Del Moray."

Carver wasn't surprised.

Beth propped her fists on her hips, stretching and arching her back so her surprisingly full breasts jutted out. He wondered if she might be trying to seduce him. It was sometimes impossible to tell with her. "Blood still runs hot in some of those retired folks," she said.

"What's that supposed to mean?"

"Sounded to me as if you took a liking to this Hattie Evans."

"Now you're thinking the way she does," he said.

A powerboat snarled past out at sea, the tone of its motor wavering whenever it bucked and its prop broke free of the waves. "I've seen some things. Maybe she's seen some of the same things. Blood runs hot in other ways, too, Fred, so you be careful."

What was she hinting at? She often seemed aware of matters he had no knowledge of, which annoyed him. Her years in the Chicago slums, her high life in Florida with Roberto, all that drug money. But it wasn't as if he hadn't seen under some rocks himself. She knew that. They never kidded each other about who was purest.

She said, "Something looks like it's gonna pop over there in retirement city, you clue me in soon as you can, okay, Fred?"

"I always do." He leaned on his cane and looked at her. The angry snarling of the speedboat had faded, and the scorching, humid quietude of the coast closed in behind it. More wind pressed in through the window, along with the whisper of surf from the beach. "There's no reason to remind me," he said. "What's wrong, you feeling insecure?"

She kissed him on the lips, barely using the tip of her tongue, stepped away, then lifted his suitcase from the bed and laid it on the floor. She placed his unpacked clothes on top of it. The surf murmured some old, old message she seemed to understand, and she smiled. Peeled off her shorts and panties and stretched out on her side on the bed. Her brown legs looked even better, fashion-model long but as muscular as a gymnast's. The dark, dark triangle in the fork of her thighs pulled at his gaze. He remembered the touch of her tongue.

She said, "C'mere, Fred. I'll show you insecure."

He hesitated a few seconds. Would it make any difference if he got into Orlando an hour or so later? He stood in the wind and sound of the ocean, mulling it over, trying not to think with his genitals. He was in love with Beth but she was a weakness. He loathed weakness in himself. Vulnerability. Christ, he loathed it!

A particularly large wave roared in and slapped and sighed on the beach.

"Fred?"

Well, it wasn't as if he had a schedule.

"Ah, Fred!"

3

SOLARTOWN WAS ten minutes outside of Orlando, a short drive off of Route 50. Carver had driven past it before but barely noticed it despite its vastness. Now he looked at it with full attention. The billboard on the highway described it as a retirement community. To Carver it looked like the first phase of the leveling process that was death.

On either side of the pale, squared stone columns that formed the entrance on Golden Drive, the pastel pink and white concrete wall surrounding Solartown stretched level in either direction, about five feet tall, with medium-size orange trees planted every hundred feet in shallow alcoves. The trees were precisely the same height. There were oranges on the ground beneath some of them. Two Latinos in blue work uniforms were picking up the oranges and dropping them into sacks strapped over their shoulders.

As he turned his ancient Olds convertible onto Golden Drive, Carver saw that the houses, like the orange trees, were all exactly the same height, the same distance apart. They were single-story ranch houses with attached double garages, shallow-pitched roofs with air-conditioning units on top, small porches, and bay windows in what were probably the dining rooms. Some of the garages were on the right, some on the left; that seemed the only difference in the houses other than color. And though colors varied, most of the clapboard-and-stucco structures were painted in pastels, with blue and pink predominating. The shingled roofs were all pale gray to reflect the sun. Most of the yards were a combination of lawn and colored gravel, and most had palms and decorative citrus trees growing in them. There were occasional lawn ornaments, from artificial flamingos and miniature windmills to religious icons. Carver drove along the flat, smooth pavement to K Street, then went east until he reached Pelican Lane, where Hattie Evans lived and grieved.

After checking house numbers, he turned right. There wasn't another car in sight, except occasionally in the shadows of garages whose doors had been left open. The heat and lack of shade made it vehicular brutality to park a car outside in the driveway or street. There were golf carts hooked up to chargers in some of the garages. Solartown's billboard had boasted of a golf course as well as a restaurant, community entertainment center, and medical facilities. One could eat, golf, and play boccie ball and never leave here right through to the end.

The way Jerome Evans had.

Carver squinted through the windshield to make sure the address number on the pale-blue house was Hattie's, then parked the Olds in the driveway. The canvas top had been up and the air conditioner blasting and it was cool in the car. When he got out and stood supported by his cane, the heat attacked him as if he'd just flung open a blast furnace door. It was the curse of air-conditioning, he decided, that when you left it the heat was doubly vicious, as if trying to make you suffer for your temporary escape.

The Olds's big engine, hot from the drive, ticked in the sun as he limped up the driveway to the small concrete porch and pressed the doorbell button with his cane. Inside the house, barely audible, Westminster chimes imitated Big Ben half a world away in a cooler clime.

After a few searing minutes even in the shade of the jutting porch roof, the door, a slightly darker blue than the rest of the house, eased open and Hattie Evans stared out at Carver.

She said, "Have you found out anything?"

"Found my way here," Carver said. He limped past her, in from the heat. "Sun's tough on us baldheaded guys."

She closed the door. "I know. My Jerome lost most of his hair twenty years ago. Virile men lose their hair earliest in life."

"That's absolutely true," Carver said, catching a sweet whiff of roses and thinking about his conversation with Beth that morning, wondering fleetingly about Hattie Evans.

He was in a small but well-furnished living room. The furniture was light oak and teak. There was a low, cream-colored sofa, a matching Lazy-Boy recliner with its footrest raised. In one corner was a tall display cabinet full of plates, not the collector kind with Norman Rockwell scenes, or likenesses of John Wayne or Elvis, but mismatched dinner and luncheon plates of elegant designs and patterns. On another wall was a bleached wood entertainment center that contained mostly books and framed photographs, but also a television with a cable box on top. It was cool in the living room. Felt good.

Hattie said, "Baby oil."

"Pardon?"

"Try baby oil on your bald head," she said. "It's good for one end and the other. Keeps you from getting sore when you're outside in the sun. Jerome used it and hardly ever wore a hat. You couldn't get that man in a hat any sooner than you could get him to wear a tie." The hard, handsome lines of her face softened as she remembered her husband.

Through the window, Carver saw a big blue Lincoln pass

like a mirage in the sun-washed street. It hadn't made a sound, and he found himself surprised he'd seen it, almost wondering if it had been real. He said, "Not much goes on around here, does it, Hattie?"

"Not out where it can be seen, anyway. This is a retirement community, so the people who run it don't encourage children or any kind of raucous behavior. A buyer has to be at least fifty-five years old to become a home or condo owner in Solartown, and the presence of children is definitely discouraged, even as guests."

"You sound as if you disagree with that policy," Carver said.

Hattie smiled sadly. "I wouldn't mind it if some nice young couple with children moved in next door. On the other hand, I understand why some residents want their hard-earned peace to remain undisturbed."

Until it merges with the peace of the grave, Carver thought, then chastised himself for being morbid.

"Contrary to what some people might believe," Hattie said, "retired schoolteachers miss children."

Carver shifted his weight more heavily over his cane and nodded. He'd have thought otherwise.

"I've forgotten my manners," Hattie said, as if surprised. "Please sit down, Mr. Carver, and I'll prepare some cool drinks. We—I have orange juice, grapefruit juice. Pepsi-Cola if you don't mind diet."

"Nothing, thanks," Carver said, not moving to sit down. "What I'd really like is for you to come with me in my car and show me around Solartown."

"If you're going to continue standing there leaving a dent in the carpet from the tip of your cane, then let's go."

She was already moving toward the door, a woman of decision and action.

Properly chastised, Carver followed.

"What exactly do you want to see?" she asked, pausing at a

closet near the door to get a navy-blue pillbox hat and plunk it on her head. Carver wondered if she wore hats because her hair was thinning.

"Oh, I just want a general view of things. So I can get a feel for the place."

"Very good, Mr. Carver." Her tone suggested she was voicing approval of his preparation for a test.

Maybe that was how she meant it exactly.

HATTIE SAT on the passenger side of the Olds's wide front seat while Carver drove. She directed him along streets with names like Reward Lane, Restful Avenue, Pension Drive. They were the north–south streets. The streets that ran east and west were lettered alphabetically.

After weaving among side streets with their middle-class, attractive but monotonous pastel houses, navigator Hattie directed Carver south on Golden Drive. They rolled past Z Street and beyond A South, B South, all the way past M South, where Golden was divided by a grassy median and widened to run toward a complex of low beige brick buildings.

"That's the community center," Hattie said. "Want to stop and look it over?"

Carver parked in front of a clean beige structure with RECREATION CENTER lettered in gold on a dark-brown sign. "Lead on," he said, turning off the engine.

She did.

He limped behind Hattie into the cool rec center. A few feet inside the glazed-glass double doors was a bulletin board with notices pinned to it announcing schedules for weaving, flower arrangement, exercise classes, literary discussion groups, swimming parties, a golf and tennis tournament. There was also a smattering of 3 × 5 cards advertising cars, golf carts, and household items for sale.

Hattie smiled and nodded hello to several gray-haired women as she led Carver along a wide, cool central corridor, past a small and busy bowling alley, past windows overlooking an Olympic-size pool where half a dozen older men and women were splashing about like kids, beyond rooms where various arts and crafts classes were in progress. Near the back of the center they stood at a floor-to-ceiling window and looked out at tennis courts, and beyond them a well-tended eighteen-hole golf course. Two golfers were jouncing on a yellow golf cart toward a distant green. On the third green, not far from where Hattie and Carver stood, a pudgy man in checked pants and a tight red pullover stood very still and studied a six-foot putt. Carver and Hattie were silent, as if their voices might disturb the golfer even at this distance and behind glass. Finally he tapped the ball neatly into the cup. Carver thought he should enter the tournament.

"Nice setup," Carver said, waving his arm in a motion that took in the rec center and outside facilities.

"That's why Jerome and I decided on this place to retire to," Hattie told him.

"Did Jerome golf?"

"Sometimes, but he wasn't a fanatic. Not like some of these retired fools who'd try to play right through a heart attack."

Beyond the trees on the far side of the course rose a circular, four-story building with a lot of windows winking in the sunlight. It seemed to be constructed of the same beige brick as the rec center. Carver asked Hattie if it was part of Solartown.

"That's our medical center," she said without emotion. "Where Jerome died."

They turned away from the view and she showed Carver the restaurant, which was like a Denny's only fancier and with more tables. "Food's not bad," she said, "and sometimes they have fashion shows here. Older male and female models wearing the kind of apparel bought by the people here in Solartown."

Apparel, Carver thought. The schoolteacher making itself

evident again in Hattie. He said, "I think I'll drop you off at home, then drive by the medical center and talk to Jerome's doctor."

"His name's Billingsly," Hattie said. "Nice young man, and reasonably competent. I'll phone and tell him you're coming and he's to confide in you about Jerome. After I talk to him he'll surely be cooperative."

"I'll just bet," Carver said.

"No lip," Hattie warned him.

Carver drove her back to her house.

Kept a civil tongue in his head.

4

AS CARVER steered the Olds into the driveway of Hattie's pastel-blue house, he noticed a man on the porch.

"Val Green," Hattie said with a trace of irritation. "He lives next door. Pesky devil."

Carver parked the car and limped beside Hattie up to the house. He was struck again by how quiet it was in Solartown. Minimum traffic noise, no voices of children. And now, in midmorning heat, not even the drone of a power mower. It wasn't going to get cooler today. Or rain. There was only unbroken blue overhead except for an airliner's high, wind-shredded vapor trail that hung in the sky like a spirit.

"Just picked up your newspaper and was setting it on the porch for you," the pesky devil named Val said to Hattie with a smile. He was a wiry little guy about seventy who had one of those faces people said would always look young, so that now it resembled a boy's face someone had penciled lines on. Carver thought he resembled Elisha Cook, Jr., the actor who was in a lot of the old black-and-white gangster films Desoto loved to watch on late-night TV.

"I'd adopt a dog if I wanted my paper fetched," Hattie told him.

His hopeful, leprechaun features fell in disappointment. Carver felt sorry for him. Hattie could be rough, all right.

"No need for a dog," Val said. "I was outside watering my lawn, so I figured I'd help out. You shouldn't be too proud to accept help, Hattie, in your stressful situation."

"Widows aren't parasites," she said. Then she seemed to remember her manners and introduced Carver to Val Green.

"I live in that green house," Val said, pointing to the pale-green house on the left of Hattie's. It was recently painted and immaculately kept. "Green like my name, so's I can always remember where I live if I was to drink too much some night." He laughed. Carver politely followed suit. Hattie somberly unlocked the door.

"Thanks," she said, as Val handed her the rolled-up newspaper.

"No trouble whatsoever. With Jerome gone, you need any heavy work done, man's work, you just call or knock on my door."

"I'll do that," Hattie said, but not with any sincerity. "Please come in, Mr. Carver."

That hadn't been in the plan, but Carver limped toward the door.

"Nice meeting you, Mr. Carver," Val said.

Carver caught a glimpse of the expression on his face as Hattie shut the door. He was sure Val was in love with Hattie. That was probably what it was about him that irritated her.

"I just wanted to give Val a chance to go home," she said. "He's difficult to be rid of when he gets talking."

"I wouldn't mind listening to him," Carver said.

"Yes you would. He can be a trial."

"He and Jerome get along?"

"Oh, sure. They'd go fishing, play cards or golf now and then. Jerome would go next door and they'd watch Braves games on TV from Atlanta. I don't like spectator sports. Or the Turner network. He colored over all those fine old movies. Sometimes Jerome and Val would watch one of those crayoned abominations."

"Aren't you being kind of tough on him?"

"Not tough enough. Anyway, he's got millions of dollars and Jane Fonda."

"I mean Val Green. He seemed a nice enough guy."

She removed her hat and sighed. "Oh, I suppose he is, at heart."

Speaking of heart. "He seems to like you a lot."

"Too much. That's the problem."

"I have to ask this," Carver said. "When Jerome was alive—"

"Val never once acted in an ungentlemanly fashion toward me," Hattie interrupted. "I will say that for him. Had he been less than honorable I would have slapped his face red and then told Jerome, and their friendship would have been terminated."

"I expect so," Carver said.

Hattie walked to the window and peeked out through the white lace curtain. "I think he's gone back in. I knew he would. It's too hot out there for an old goat like him."

"Safe for me to go, then," Carver told her. He limped to the door and opened it. "I'll call if I learn anything. If you want me, leave a message at the Warm Sands Motel. I've got a room reserved there, but I haven't checked in yet."

"That place has a reputation," Hattie said.

It took Carver a few seconds to realize what she meant. "It would anyway," Carver told her, "being near a retirement community."

Hattie seemed to find nothing incongruous in that observation as she saw him out.

Val hadn't gone inside. He was standing in his front yard watering his lawn with a green hose equipped with a complicated brass nozzle.

As Carver was about to get in the Olds, Val did something to the nozzle that stopped the flow of water, then walked over to him. He moved stiffly yet with a spry kind of nimbleness, as if his legs were still strong out of proportion to his thin frame. Carver leaned with his forearm on the open car door and waited for him.

"Wanted to talk to you alone," Val said, when he'd gotten near enough for there to be no chance he might be overheard inside the house. "There's a few things you need to understand about Hattie."

Carver hoped she wasn't watching through the window; he understood that much about her.

"She's plenty broke up about Jerome's passing," Val said.

"That's natural. He was her husband."

"But it don't mean she ain't thinking straight in being suspicious about how he died."

"She tell you she had suspicions?"

"Didn't have to tell me. I can read her."

"What do you think?" Carver asked. "You knew Jerome."

"Knew him, all right. He seemed a healthy one. I didn't figure him for a heart attack."

"You think he died from one?"

"I don't see how it coulda been anything else, but somehow it don't set right. That's why I wanted to tell you, you need my help for anything just ask. I'm a member of the Posse."

"Posse?"

"The Solartown Posse." Val pointed to his garage. The overhead door was raised and the rear bumper of the green Dodge

Aries parked inside sported a sticker that said just that: SO-
LARTOWN POSSE.

"What's the Solartown Posse?" Carver asked.

"We're an auxiliary of the Orlando Police Department. Solartown's in their jurisdiction, but we're out far enough from
the center of town we're kinda isolated, so we run our own
civilian patrols. We ain't armed, but we got radios, and we keep
an eye on things and phone in for the law if we see a crime going
down. We're the eyes and ears of the law, you might say."

Or might not, Carver thought, considering the eyesight and
hearing of a senior citizens' patrol. On the other hand, their
seasoned judgment might far outweigh any physical disadvan-
tages. It was easier to see things in shades of gray once your
hair had made the transition.

"I'll keep your offer in mind," Carver said. "But how did you
know I might be looking into the circumstances of Jerome's
death?"

"Hattie's been talking about hiring someone, and I figured
you was it. No offense, but you got cop written on your forehead.
And I seen your bum leg and figured you wasn't active in the
department, so I thought you was probably private. I was right,
wasn't I?" He arched pointy gray eyebrows. "Wasn't I?" he
repeated.

Carver said he was.

"That being the case," Val said, "I advise you to go talk to
Maude Crane. Lives over on the corner of Beach and G Street."

"Hattie didn't mention her."

"She wouldn't. Maude and Jerome was more'n a little
friendly. You understand my meaning?"

"Sure. But how do you know it's true?"

"Jerome told a few of us when we had too much to drink
after a round of golf one day. Bragged, is what he did. No
gentleman, Jerome. Thing is, Hattie didn't know about any of

it. I wouldn't want her to find out now. There wouldn't be no use in it, only pain for her."

"I doubt she'll need to know," Carver said.

"Good. I'm on night patrol for a while. You need me anytime after eleven, call that number on my bumper sticker. That's headquarters. They'll get a hold of me on the radio."

"I'll do that," Carver said. He lowered himself into the Olds. The afternoon was still glaringly bright and hot. Carver's shirt became glued to his back immediately when he settled into the sticky vinyl upholstery. His bald pate was throbbing. Val didn't seem to feel the heat.

"I don't wanna see Hattie get hurt any more'n is necessary," Val said.

"I can see that."

Val stepped back, and Carver shut the car door and started the engine.

He backed out into the street and saw that Val had returned to watering his lawn. There seemed to be someone standing behind the front curtains in Hattie's house, but Carver couldn't be sure. The sunlight glancing off the glass made seeing inside difficult. He put the Olds in drive.

There was plenty of time to see Dr. Billingsly at the medical center. Right now, he was anxious to meet Maude Crane.

He drove toward the corner of Beach and G Street, not liking the direction matters had taken, but amused and buoyed by the knowledge that infatuation could strike at any age.

5

MAUDE CRANE's house was exactly the shade of pastel green as Val's. Made Carver wonder.

The house was angled on a wide corner lot strewn with small citrus trees, most of which bore oranges or grapefruits. Some of the fruit lay rotting on the ground. The drapes were closed on all the windows except for the standard bay window in the dining room, and there appeared to be a large potted indoor plant before that window that blocked the view out or in.

Carver sat in the parked Olds and studied the house. After a while in his business, you developed an instinct. There was something about the house that didn't feel right.

Then he realized what it was. There was mail visible in the box by the door, and the screen door was slightly ajar, as if the postman had run out of room in the box and had been stuffing mail inside the outer door.

As he planted his cane and levered himself up out of the Olds, Carver noticed that the grass, though of uniform height, needed mowing. He limped across the sunbaked lawn in a path directly to the porch, each step raising a cloud of tiny insects, a few of which found their way up his pants legs to where his ankles were bare above his socks. The yard was as unyielding beneath the tip of his cane as if it were concrete; it hadn't been watered for a long time. There was a medium-size sugar oak near the corner of the house, its leaves perforated until they'd been turned into fine lace by insects. Florida in the summer belonged to the bugs.

His suspicion was confirmed. The space between the screen door and the green-enameled front door was stuffed with mail. Bills, advertising circulars, a few letters. There was a scattering of small, glossy mail-order catalogs. A pretty blond woman squeezing some kind of exercise device between her thighs was on one cover, smiling up at Carver as if she might be doing something naughty.

There was a brass knocker shaped like a lion's head on the door. Carver banged it loudly and waited. He wasn't surprised when there was no response. The lion roared at him silently.

He stood on the porch and glanced around. There was no one in sight. He felt like the only living and moving figure in a painting. The orderly retirement community might as well have featured crypts instead of houses.

He chastised himself for the thought. Get up in your sixties, seventies, or older, it was apparently silence and order you preferred. That was how it seemed to work. He'd know for sure soon enough.

The slam of a door made him turn.

A woman had emerged from the house next door. She was heavy and trudged with effort but determination, wearing paint-smeared white overalls and carrying a screwdriver. A pair of rimless glasses rode low on her wide nose and she squinted over them in the bright sunlight. Her bulldog features tried a smile but it only made her uglier as she got near Carver.

"You David?" she asked.

Carver shook his head no.

The woman seemed to have known he wasn't really David, but she said, "Thought you might be David Crane from Atlanta. Maude's nephew. She was expecting him. I'm Mildred Klein from next door. Some way I can help you?"

"I was looking for Maude Crane."

"I figured that, you being on her porch and all."

Ah, the neighbors watching out for one another. The old tended to band close together like any other minority group. The paranoia wasn't completely unjustified.

"Do you know where I can find her?"

"Maybe she drove on into Orlando to shop," Mildred said. "She does that now and again." Her grip on the screwdriver's yellow plastic handle tightened, as if she were ready to use it as a weapon if necessary. "You selling something?"

"No, I'm—" Carver suddenly became aware of a sound that had been on the edge of his consciousness, like something electrical buzzing inside the house. "You hear that?"

"Hear what?"

Carver put his ear to the door. The buzzing was louder. He moved away and leaned on his cane, motioning for Mildred to listen.

Without taking her gaze from him, she mimicked his actions at the door, pressing her ear close to the wood. She nodded, puzzled. "I hear. Something running in there."

"Maybe an electric alarm clock," Carver said.

"Maybe." But Mildred seemed doubtful. It didn't really sound like an alarm clock.

"We should look," Carver said.

"None of our business."

"If Maude left something on, you can turn it off. I'll wait out here."

"What makes you think I can get in?"

"I figure you're her closest neighbor, and you came over here looking out for her, so maybe she gave you a key in case of emergency."

"You see this as an emergency?"

Carver stirred the clutter of mail with his cane. The girl with the exerciser between her thighs smiled up at him, trying to reassure him there was nothing in the world worth his worry. "Maude mention to you she was taking a trip?"

Mildred looked uncertain, sliding her glasses higher on her sweat-glistening nose as if to see Carver better. They immediately slid back down. "She usually tells me when she's gonna be gone more'n a day," she admitted.

Carver said again, "I'll wait out here if you want."

Mildred hefted the screwdriver in her hand. "Who'd you say you were?"

"My name's Fred Carver. I'm working for a woman named Hattie Evans."

Something shadowed Mildred's face. She'd heard of Hattie. "Don't know her," she said.

"I need to talk to Maude," he said simply. "Maybe she's sick in there and hasn't been able to get to the door or phone. It happens, doesn't it?"

"It happens." She glared at him as if sizing him up finally, then moved over a few feet and stooped down and picked up one of several rocks lining the flower bed near the porch. It was about six inches in diameter. Apparently she'd found him wanting and decided to crush him.

But instead of hurling the rock at Carver, she opened it like a hinged box and removed a key.

"Looks real, don't it?" she said, as she replaced the now obviously lightweight fake rock.

"Fooled me." He stood back as she unlocked the door and shoved it open, poking her head inside to yell for Maude Crane.

Immediately she backed reeling out onto the porch, as if someone had punched her in the face. The screwdriver clattered on the concrete floor and she stood gaping at Carver, sickened and terrified.

He caught a whiff of the stench that had struck her like something solid.

Mildred tried to speak but no sound emerged, only a string of saliva that glistened on her chin in the sun. Carver helped her walk twenty feet away from the door, where she sat down with her legs spread wide on the hard ground and vomited.

After a while, he rested his hand on her damp back. "You gonna be all right?"

She nodded, staring at the mess on the grass between her legs. Her glasses had somehow gotten spotted.

"Don't try to get up," he said. "I'll be right back."

Another nod.

He set the tip of his cane and limped toward the open door, a metallic taste at the edges of his tongue.

Ten feet away he took a deep breath and held it, then quickened his pace. He shoved the mail aside with his cane and hobbled into the house.

The air-conditioning was off and the place was even hotter than outside. In here, the faint buzzing he'd heard on the porch was a din, with a frantic rising and falling pitch. This time of year especially in Florida, he knew what it was.

A dark cloud of flies swarmed relentlessly in the center of the dining room, feeding on something dangling from the chandelier.

The something was Maude Crane.

6

CARVER PARKED the Olds in the wide lot of the medical center the next day and limped toward the circular four-story buff building. The morning sun pressed hotly on his shoulders and he knew the top of his head was getting burned. Virility could be a burden. Maybe he'd have to borrow one of Hattie's lids.

When he got inside the building, he saw the practicality of its architecture. On each floor, the rooms were off short halls leading like spokes from a hub that was the nurses' station, so that each patient was only steps and seconds away from the healing hands of mercy.

The elevator reached the fourth-floor offices, and he limped out and told a redheaded receptionist at a long curved desk he'd like to talk to Dr. Billingsly. She smiled and asked him to please have a seat, which he did, for almost an hour.

Just as he reached the very brink of Muzak madness, a short, stocky young man wearing a wrinkled green surgical gown and cap entered the waiting area and smiled at Carver. He didn't look old enough to be a doctor, which made Carver wonder how old *he* might look to Dr. Billingsly.

"William Billingsly," he said, shaking hands firmly with Carver. He had blond hair and a smoothly chubby and intelligent face with shrewd blue eyes, like a grown-up cherub who'd somehow figured it all out. "Mrs. Evans phoned and told me you were coming by."

Carver said he wanted to talk with Billingsly about Jerome Evans, and the doctor said, "Sure," and led him to a tiny waiting room equipped with a small sofa, three chairs, and a TV jutting from the wall on an elbowed metal bracket. There was also a Mr. Coffee on a table in a corner, its round glass pot almost full. The wallpaper looked like burlap. Carver noticed that Billingsly sneaked a glance at his wristwatch as they sat down, Carver in a brown vinyl Danish chair, the doctor on the beige sofa. It was cool and quiet in the room.

"I don't think we'll be disturbed here," Billingsly said.

"I'd have gotten here sooner after Hattie Evans's phone call," Carver told him, "except for Maude Crane."

At first Billingsly didn't seem to know what Carver was talking about. Then it registered in his canny blue eyes. "Ah! You know about that."

"I'm the one who discovered her body."

"Ah!" Billingsly looked over at Mr. Coffee and pointed. His hands were small, with stubby, manicured fingers. "Care for a cup, Mr. Carver?"

Carver told him no thanks, then watched as Billingsly got up and poured himself some coffee, tore open a paper packet and added powdered cream that had probably never known a cow, and sat back down. "I'm afraid suicide's all too common here in Solartown, as it is in all retirement communities of this size. The old get despondent." He took a sip of coffee and made a face as if it didn't taste good. "Sometimes I don't blame them."

"How long had Maude Crane been dead?" Carver asked.

Billingsly shook his head. "I wasn't present when she was brought here, only heard about it. They say several days. Death by hanging, and with an electrical cord. Asphyxiation, accompanying severe subcutaneous and cartilage trauma. The family wants an autopsy, which will be performed tomorrow. Then more will be known, but I'd guess not much more. Suicides by hanging are rather obvious. Discoloration, ruptured eye capillaries. The indications were observable, even with the damage inflicted by the flies and the heat."

"Do you know as much about Jerome Evans's death?"

Billingsly smiled boyishly at his coffee. "Oh, yes. I was his personal physician, in the operating room when he expired."

"Hattie Evans said he died at home at the kitchen table."

"For all practical purposes, she's right. But there were still faint vital signs when he was brought in. Nothing could have been done for him, Mr. Carver."

"Did you sign the death certificate?"

"No. Dr. Wynn, our chief surgeon and hospital administrator, signed it, as he signs most death certificates. He was in the O.R. at the time of death, too."

"Hattie Evans has doubts about her husband dying of a heart attack."

"I've heard her express those doubts. And I can understand why she might feel that way, since he had no history of coronary problems. But I saw the evidence, and it was classic. A massive blockage resulting in fibrillation and rupture of the aorta. In other words, a heart attack brought on by a blood clot. The postmortem confirmed that beyond doubt."

"Is something like that common in a patient Jerome's age?"

"All too common, coronary history or not. Mr. Carver, we have only so much time on this earth, and some of us have more difficulty than others accepting when it runs out for us or those

| 31 |

we love. Believe me, Jerome Evans's death was caused by a massive coronary. I've seen it before, and I'll probably see it again within the next few weeks. And, like poor Mrs. Evans, the widow will wonder how it could have happened. For a while she might resist believing it."

"Resist as strongly as Hattie Evans?"

Billingsly smiled again. "Ah! Mrs. Evans is a strong woman." He took a long pull of coffee and glanced at his watch. "I like her, which is why I was glad to agree to talk with you. To reassure her that, like so many other women in this land of dietary idiocy, she lost her husband to a heart attack. It's cruel, but it's simple reality. She'll simply have to adapt, and I'm sure she will." He stood up and drained his foam cup, then tossed it into a plastic-lined wastebasket near the coffee machine. Another discard whose time had run out.

Carver planted his cane and stood, also. He thanked Billingsly for his time.

"Tell Mrs. Evans I said hello," the doctor told Carver, as he bustled out of the waiting room. Carver watched him hurry down the hall and disappear beyond the busy, circular counter that was the nurses' station. One of the nurses glanced after Billingsly, then at another nurse, and both women smiled.

Carver poured himself a cup of coffee and sat back down, watching a gray and withered man in an oversized blue robe shuffle along the hall while pushing a portable steel stand with a transparent envelope dangling from it. The sack of clear liquid was joined to the back of his hand by a coiled plastic tube and an IV needle.

The old get despondent, the wise young Dr. Billingsly had said.

Maybe Hattie Evans clung to her craving for justice rather than sink into that despondency after her husband's sudden and unexpected death. She was a willful woman who would cling fiercely and not be easily dislodged. Definitely the last-leaf-upon-the-tree type.

Obsession was preferable to suicide. Carver knew that.

Maybe that explained it all, he thought, watching the old man with the portable IV disappear into one of the rooms.

Or maybe it explained nothing.

| 7 |

"EXPLAIN," Desoto said.

Carver was sitting in front of Lieutenant Alfonso Desoto's desk in his office on Hughey in Orlando. Desoto was elegantly dressed as usual. Pale-gray suit, mauve shirt with maroon tie, gold watch, two gold rings, gold cuff links. On him it somehow didn't look flashy. He had the dark and classic looks of a matinee idol in one of the old movies he loved, the one where the handsome bullfighter gets the girl. Those who didn't know him sometimes guessed he was a gigolo rather than a tough cop. That could be a serious mistake.

Carver explained the connection between Hattie Evans and the late Maude Crane. To wit: the late Jerome Evans.

Desoto leaned back in his chair and flashed his cuff links. Behind him, a Sony portable on the windowsill was playing sad Latin guitar music very softly. "What you're saying, *amigo*, is that someone might have murdered Maude Crane?"

"Not exactly," Carver said. "I guess what I'm doing is asking."

"If what you say is true about Crane's affair with Jerome Evans, and Crane was murdered, the prime suspect would be Hattie Evans, your client."

"Even with Jerome dead?"

"The need for vengeance doesn't die with the prize," Desoto said. The breeze from the air conditioner barely ruffled his sleek black hair. Carver couldn't remember ever seeing Desoto's hair seriously mussed.

"I don't even know if Hattie was aware of her husband's affair, having only heard about it secondhand myself."

"Secondhand from whom?"

"Her next-door neighbor, Val Green."

"How would he know?"

"He gets around. He's a member of the Solartown Posse."

Desoto absently buffed the ring on his right hand on the left sleeve of his suit coat. The guitar on the Sony was strummed suddenly in swift, dramatic tempo. "That's the civilian volunteer group that patrols the place, hey?"

"That's it," Carver said. He thought Desoto might scoff at the Posse, but he didn't. Volunteer groups—some might call them vigilante groups—were becoming more and more prevalent as the war on drugs drained law enforcement of resources. The police were beginning to see the good ones as an asset. The bad ones could be the worst kind of liability. "I'm not sure about Val Green, so I'm not sure Jerome and Maude were actually seeing each other behind Hattie's back."

"Be sure," Desoto said. "It was in the suicide note."

He opened a file folder on his desk and handed Carver a sheet of white paper. Carver rested his cane on his thigh and read. Typed on the cheap white bond paper was a long, pathetic account of how lonely Maude Crane's life had become, and how she'd prefer death over living without Jerome. Above her typed name was an indecipherable ink scrawl.

Carver laid the note faceup on the desk. His hip was getting numb; he had to shift his weight, move his bad leg. "Anyone might have typed this."

"But they didn't."

"And the signature could have been made by somebody flinging ink from across the room."

"But it wasn't. The paper was still in Maude Crane's Smith-Corona manual typewriter, and her prints and hers alone were on the keys. The signature, vague as it is, matches samples we found among her personal papers. This one is suicide plain and simple, *amigo*. And the second one this year in Solartown. Sometimes the very old, the very sick and sad, choose it as their way out, hey? You should understand that."

Carver knew what he meant. It was Desoto who'd helped to prevent him from one day swimming out to sea too far to return, when he was depressed after taking disability retirement from the department with his maimed leg. The reference to past agony irritated Carver. He said, "Why did you send Hattie Evans to me?"

Desoto smiled. He loved women as much as they loved him. Any age, race, nationality. The faded but defiant spirit of Hattie Evans might have gotten to him, caused him to regard her as something more than just another suspicious and fearful old woman. "I liked her, *amigo*. But more than that, I didn't think she was the type to become paranoid in her old age. Maybe the facts didn't warrant me sending her to you; they certainly didn't warrant a police investigation. Still, I felt there might be something real in what she was saying. Call it more of a character judgment than anything else."

Carver tapped the rubber tip of his cane soundlessly on the floor, staring at it and nodding. Cops' instincts. They should be given more official standing. "I picked up the same quality in her," he said.

"You going to tell her about Maude Crane's affair with her husband?"

"I don't want to," Carver said. "That's why I came here, to reassure myself there's no connection between Jerome Evans's death and Maude Crane's, other than the emotional linkage."

"There's no other connection," Desoto assured Carver. "This part of the game is exactly as it seems. An old woman lost her husband, another her lover and companion and then her will to live. A world of fighters and quitters. Don't put the widow, the one survivor of the triangle, through unnecessary pain." His dark eyes were somber, full of genuine sympathy for Hattie Evans. So unlike a cop sometimes.

Carver stared at the suicide note on Desoto's desk, listening to the sounds of the policeman's world wafting into the office between the notes of the sad Spanish guitar. Gruff voices, sometimes joking; the faint chatter of a police radio; the shrill protests of a suspect being booked. There seemed no need for Hattie to know anything other than what she might read in the newspaper or catch on TV news. Another soul, old and alone in Solartown, had chosen the time and means of deliverance.

"No reason to tell Hattie about the affair," Carver said. "I'll see it as a suicide for now."

"Then you're seeing it as it is, *amigo*. It shouldn't get in the way of your job. Am I right?"

"Sure," Carver said.

But he wasn't sure.

HE DROVE from the Municipal Justice Building on Hughey back to Solartown and rang Hattie's doorbell.

She'd been cleaning. As she ushered him into her cool and orderly living room, he saw a canister vacuum cleaner with a pythonlike hose and attachments resting in the doorway between dining room and kitchen. Hattie was wearing an old gray blouse and a calf-length blue skirt. Carver wondered if she ever wore slacks. Ever cursed like a sailor. Masturbated.

"Getting things straightened up," she explained, as she sat down on the sofa opposite Carver, who'd set his cane and lowered himself into a chair. He wondered if she meant her house or her life. He was aware of the acrid scent of just-vacuumed carpet, and there were parallel tracks in the plush pile of the living room. The dishwasher was running, and the soapy fragrance of perfumed detergent drifted from the kitchen. Underlying it all was the subtle scent of roses.

"I talked to Dr. Billingsly," he said, "and he assured me there was nothing unusual about Jerome's coronary, either statistically or from what he observed in the operating room."

Hattie nodded distractedly. It was unlike her not to focus in. "Yes, Dr. Billingsly mentioned to me he was present when Jerome's official death occurred." She brushed back a wisp of thinning gray hair and suddenly stared directly at Carver. Her seamed, chiseled features would have been a credit to Mount Rushmore. "I heard on the news about Maude Crane's suicide."

Carver didn't know quite what to say, so he merely nodded.

She said, "Suicide, my eye, young man!"

"Why do you say that?" Treading carefully.

"I know about her affair with my husband, Mr. Carver. Known about it for years."

Carver decided that sounded right. Not much got past Hattie. "Was Jerome aware that you knew?"

She gave him an incredulous look. "Of course not."

"I've talked to the police, and to Billingsly, about Maude Crane's death. They're calling it suicide."

"*They* can be wrong. They're not infallible."

"Are you?"

"I come closer."

Carver leaned forward in his chair, both hands folded over the crook of his cane. "Hattie, if you did manage to convince the police the Crane woman's death wasn't suicide, you'd be the prime suspect."

"Well, maybe I killed her."

"Not likely."

"You don't think I'm capable of such a thing?"

"I think you're too logical."

She smiled in a way he liked. "I've always taken pride in my ability to do whatever's necessary in any situation."

"Me, too," Carver said.

"I sensed that in you. That's why I hired you. I also assume you're smart enough to see that my killing Maude Crane would have been in no way necessary. Before Jerome died, maybe. Certainly not now."

"She killed herself," Carver said, not sure if he believed it. "I saw the suicide note."

"Did it tell about her and Jerome?"

"Yeah, so the police know about the affair, and your possible motive."

"I don't blame Jerome for the affair," Hattie said. "Did the note say something about his cold and unresponsive wife?"

"Words to that effect," Carver admitted.

"Hmph! Well, Jerome had his reasons to stray, and perhaps sex was one of them. But we were married forty-three years, Mr. Carver. That creates bonds that couldn't be broken by Jerome occasionally having his way with some lonely widow in the dark. Maude Crane was a fool if she believed otherwise, like foolish other women down through time."

"People not married forty-three years might not understand that," Carver said.

"Do you?"

"I'll take your word for it."

"I'm in some ways responsible for the furtive and disgusting extramarital affair, and if I thought Maude Crane actually killed herself, I'd feel partly responsible for her death."

Carver didn't want to hurt her even more deeply, but he decided he'd better lay out the cards faceup for her. "You're telling me you think Jerome's and Maude Crane's deaths were murder, which would mean there's some kind of conspiracy. But what evidence there is points in the opposite direction. You've got to realize the police will write your ideas off as the suspicious nature that often accompanies advanced age."

"You mean they'll figure me for an addle-brained, paranoid old woman."

"Well, yes."

"I hired you to think otherwise. Do you?"

He grinned. Hattie wasn't one to hesitate laying down her own cards faceup. "Yeah, I think otherwise, or I wouldn't be letting you spend your money on my services. But I have to tell you, I'm not as sure as you are that there's something irregular going on."

"Was the Crane woman's suicide note handwritten?"

"No, it was typed and signed in pen."

"Hmph!"

Carver sighed.

Hattie said, "Keep digging, Mr. Carver. You're an honorable man and you'll earn your money. That's all I ask."

"I'll pick up the threads and follow them," Carver told her, "but I can't guarantee you'll like where they lead."

"If they lead to the truth, Mr. Carver, I'll be satisfied. Now, would you like a glass of lemonade?"

Carver told her yes, that would be fine, and they sat in her screened-in "Florida room" attached to the back of the house and sipped lemonade from tall frosted glasses.

"Freshly squeezed fruit from my own trees," Hattie told him with satisfaction.

He wasn't surprised to find it unsweetened.

8

THE WARM SANDS MOTEL, where Carver had made reservations, was just off the Orange Blossom Trail, miles from the nearest ocean. But it had an artificial white sand beach surrounding a small lake, and it was built of artificial driftwood so it looked as if someone shipwrecked and with carpenter skills had built it. Someone high on fermented mangoes.

Despite the rustic exterior, Carver's room was what might be called castaway luxurious, with crude-looking but expensive driftwood-gray dresser, desk, and headboard, and Winslow Homer seascape prints on the walls. The room had plush gray carpet and heavy, sea-blue drapes that matched the bedspread. From his window he could see the small kidney-shape swimming pool with several tanned and weary-looking adults lounging about on webbed chairs as if the sun had drugged them. He could hear but not see children playing in the lake and in the sand that had been trucked in.

He pulled the drapes closed, then undressed and took a long, lukewarm shower. After toweling off with rough terry cloth, he got his cane from where it was leaning against the toilet tank and limped back into the cool room. He put on Levi's, gray sweat socks, and soft brown moccasins, a gray pullover shirt with a pocket for his sunglasses. Then he limped back into the bathroom and brushed his hair, studied himself in the mirror and decided he looked like the same guy only a shade older. That was okay; he had no illusions about time. His bald pate was deeply tanned and a little tender, but it didn't seem as if it would peel. Reasonably satisfied with his mirror image, he left the room and limped outside and down past the office to the Warm Sands Seagrill Cafe for an early supper. Compensation for having skipped lunch.

After the swordfish steak dinner and two cups of coffee, he went outside and wrestled an *Orlando Sentinel* from a vending machine. He sat on a bench in the shade, listening to the kids screech and splash down on the artificial beach by the artificial lake while he read about real violence all over the world. Seen as part of the big picture, Jerome Evans's death seemed relatively unimportant. Which Carver supposed it was—except to Hattie Evans.

Mosquitoes found him, notified the rest of the squadron, and began to go to work on him, sometimes seeming to attack in formation. But he doggedly read on, checking the sports page to see how the Braves did last night, scanning the comics section to see how Charlie Brown was doing in his running conflict with Lucy. They'd both lost.

When he was finished with the paper, he limped back into his room, sat on the edge of the bed with the phone in his lap, and called Beth.

"I need you to do something for me," he said, when she'd picked up in Del Moray.

"Sure you do, Fred," she said in a husky voice. "You miss me already."

"That all you think about?"

"No, but I think about it a lot."

"Think about using the resources of *Burrow* and your own limitless resourcefulness to do some research for me. Might involve some computer work. That possible?"

"My, my. Butter wouldn't melt."

"Will you do it?"

"Sure. *Burrow*'s got computer people working for them who make NASA seem like hackers. What you need to know? How to get the Ninja Turtles past all those obstacles?"

He listened to the voices of the young from down at the beach. Listened to the rush of traffic over on the Orange Blossom Trail, not so unlike the eternal sigh of the sea. "I need to know how the death rate at Solartown compares with the rates at similar retirement communities."

She was silent for a moment. Then she said, "It'd all be public record, in state data banks. It's the kind of information Jeff could come up with."

"Jeff?"

"Jeff Mehling, computer guy at *Burrow*. He's part microchip himself."

"How long would it take this Jeff to do the job?"

"Nanoseconds, if he knows what keys to punch. He's hooked into the office with his home computer, so I can probably call you back with the information tonight."

Carver told her he'd be waiting, she should take as many nanoseconds as she needed.

"There a story in this for *Burrow*?" she asked. "That'd be part of the bargain."

"*Our* bargain?"

"It's what Clive'll ask." Clive Jones was the founder and managing editor of *Burrow*, an intrepid former ACLU lawyer who wore conservative business suits while riding a motorcycle with suicidal abandon. "What should I tell him?"

"Say that if there's a story, you'll be the one to get it."

"What Clive'll say, Fred, is that I oughta be where you are, covering this thing firsthand."

"There's nothing yet to cover with any hand."

"But there will be, right?" She was like a radar-homed missile.

"My sense of it is there will be," he admitted. "Why don't you drive here tomorrow, meet me at the motel about noon."

"So, you need my help in more ways than one."

"Many more ways."

"You need many ways, I got 'em."

"I miss you," he said, scratching a mosquito bite.

"That all you think about?"

He said, "No, but I think about it a lot."

"We got a lunch date," she said, and broke the connection.

He hung up the phone and stretched out on his back on the bed, thinking about it.

THE ROOM was dark when the phone's persistent ringing hauled him up from deep sleep.

The first thing he realized was that he had an erection. The second was that his head throbbed with pain each time the phone jangled. The second realization had taken care of the first by the time he'd dragged the receiver to him and mumbled a hello.

"You been sleepin', Fred?"

Beth.

He shook his head, trying to rattle sleep from his brain. "Just resting my eyes." The room was cool and dim. He peered at the glowing red numerals on the TV clock radio: 10:30. "Jesus!"

"Whazza matter, lover?"

"Didn't realize it was so late."

"Well, you gave your eyes a good long rest. Other parts of

you might get tired, but those eyes are probably good for all night."

Carver was awake enough now to be irritated. "You call to aggravate me, or do you have that information?"

"Called 'cause I'm doing you a favor, remember?"

"Yeah, I recollect." He switched on the lamp, wincing as the light assailed his eyes. "Sorry."

"You're a bear when you first wake up, Fred."

He waited in bearish silence. There was a terrible taste in his mouth. Possibly the fur on his teeth.

"Jeff accessed various data banks, did some checking and cross-checking. He worked this out on a per-capita basis, deaths per thousand people in various age groups. Compared to other retirement communities in Florida, California, and Arizona, the Solartown death rate is nine-point-eight percent higher across the board."

"Across the board? That mean in every age group?"

"Jeff said there's less than a three-tenths of a percent difference in the rates within age groups. Of course, the higher the age bracket, the more annual deaths per thousand residents."

Carver didn't know what to think. "That seem reasonable, that nine-point-eight percent difference?"

"Jeff thought it was high, but within the realm of a statistical fluke. Might mean something or nothing. In Solartown, out of a population of over four thousand, there were two hundred twenty natural deaths. So you've got an extra twenty-one-point-something people died there over the average. That mean anything to your investigation, Fred?"

"Not necessarily. It doesn't mean there's a serial killer operating in Solartown, but it doesn't mean there isn't. It might simply have been a bad year for fatalities."

"Bad couple of years. These figures cover twenty-four months."

"Jeff's thorough. Tell him I said thanks."

"Sure. Remember our lunch date."

Carver assured her he would, then hung up. He lay back down on the bed but left the light on. It would be interesting to know how many of Solartown's 220 deaths last year were due to heart attacks, and how many of them were male. How many widows were created.

It was time to talk with Dr. Arthur Wynn at the medical center.

Rather, it would be time tomorrow. Carver knew he had a better chance of meeting the subject of a séance than convincing a medical doctor to talk with him at ten-forty in the evening.

He dragged the phone over to him and rested it on his chest. Remembering the number on the POSSE bumper sticker on Val Green's car, he pecked it out with his forefinger.

An elderly female voice told him which part of Solartown Val was patrolling.

Carver thanked her, then replaced the phone, got up, and went into the bathroom. He rinsed his face, brushed his teeth, then limped outside into the warm night to where the Olds was parked.

He wanted to find out what Val Green had to say away from Hattie's presence and influence.

Val was doubtless an honorable and tight-lipped man, but Carver was reasonably sure he could bribe him with free coffee and doughnuts. Make him feel like a real cop.

9

VAL INVITED Carver to park his car and ride with him on patrol. "It'll be a quiet night," Val promised, "like all the rest of 'em."

Carver lowered himself into the passenger's side of Val's five-year-old green Dodge and rested his cane between his legs. The car's air conditioner worked well. There was a CB radio mounted below the dash with a microphone hooked into a bracket. The Dodge was a stick shift. Val let it wind out in first gear, then shifted with a *clunk!* and a jerk into second, then almost immediately into third. The little car whined but responded peppily to this abuse.

"Gotta keep an eye out over on N Street," Val said, glancing at Carver from the corner of his vision. The glow of the dashboard lights made the white of his eye gleam. "There was a spate of vandalism over there last week. Woman reported her citrus trees bent, all the fruit on the ground."

Sounds serious, Carver thought, if you're an orange.

"Kids from the city, way I figure it," Val said. "Come cruising through here now and then, mostly looking for something to do. Don't generally amount to much, but it's the kinda thing's gotta be contained."

Carver said, "You like doughnuts?"

"Yeah, but I don't make it a habit to eat while I'm on duty."

"I thought you guys would have uniforms," Carver said, looking at Val's white slacks and green golf shirt. And he was wearing white slip-on shoes that looked like house slippers. Not good for chasing bad guys.

Val smiled, staring straight ahead. "Maybe this *is* the uniform."

"Okay," Carver said, "I'm sorry if I seem to be taking the Posse lightly. Desoto said you people did good work."

"Who's he?"

"Homicide lieutenant in Orlando."

Val slowed to five miles an hour for a stop sign, *clunk*ed the Dodge into second gear, and regained speed. The houses slipped by on either side of the car, all of identical height and architecture, like the same house over and over; might have been an Andy Warhol poster. "Desoto the one Hattie went to about Jerome?" Val asked.

"Right."

Carver said nothing while Val slowed the car and looked to the side at a shirtless, white-haired man picking up something from a dark lawn. The man saw the car, waved, and ambled back inside the house carrying a rolled-up newspaper. "I drove over to talk to Maude Crane like you suggested," Carver said. "I found her dead."

Val made a left turn and nodded. "Heard it on the news, that she went and hung herself. Wasn't surprised. Guilt and loneliness, if it wasn't murder."

"What makes you think murder?"

"I done some talking with Hattie, and I kinda agree with her it don't seem logical Jerome'd just keel over with a heart attack."

"I thought we were talking about Maude Crane."

"Talking about her and Jerome."

Val's concentration tended to slip off the track occasionally. Carver decided it was a good thing the Posse wasn't armed.

"Suicides happen frequently in retirement communities," Carver said. "So do heart attacks."

"Not to Jerome. He was a healthy guy, strong and fulla piss and vinegar. Popular with most everybody, 'specially the ladies. Jerome didn't sleep sometimes at night, so he roamed around the house, sometimes woke up Hattie. Living next door like I do, I heard things. I didn't like him much, considering how he treated Hattie."

"He mistreated her?"

"Ordered her around like dirt, is what he did. Then of course he had his thing on the side with Maude Crane."

"Did he know Hattie knew about Maude?"

Val rubbed his chin and held the Dodge at about five miles an hour on the deserted street. Most of the houses were dark. Bedtime was early in Solartown. "He probably knew and didn't care. Nothing I know was said about it by either of them. Married man getting some strange on the side, and with a wife like Hattie, it sure ain't right. She let it go on. She let too many things go on with Jerome. It's a terrible thing to say, but myself, I think it's better for her in her remaining years that he's passed on. And if she could settle in her mind the suspicions about his death, she could forget him and move on with her life. End the chapter, sorta. You think?"

Carver said he did, he thought so. Which was why he was working for Hattie.

He sat silently for a while as they followed the grid of dark streets. Then he said, "You know, if anybody really believed Maude Crane was murdered, Hattie'd be the prime suspect."

Val tromped a floppy white shoe down on the brake pedal. Carver had to brace with a palm against the dash to keep from hitting the windshield. As the car stopped rocking, he grabbed his cane and held it.

"Hattie killing anyone is a ridiculous idea!" Val said angrily. "Her exact problem is she's too kind and considerate. I spent time in Korea, Carver. I knew killers. There's something about them, and Hattie's not one of them."

"I don't see her that way, either," Carver said, though he'd known killers who would have fooled Val. Who'd fooled everyone for a long time, including their victims.

Mollified, Val slipped the Dodge into gear and goosed it up to ten miles an hour, shifted choppily to second, and held that speed as the motor lugged along like an asthmatic.

"We're talking about two victims, if you include Maude Crane," Carver said. "And maybe more. You hinting there might be a serial killer operating in Solartown?"

Val didn't seem taken aback by the idea. "Well, I never considered it, but it's possible. Generally, though, they use knives or guns, don't they?"

"Generally. But there are ways to induce heart attacks. The Russians have done it chemically for years. Maybe even the C.I.A. Any former C.I.A. operatives living in Solartown?"

"Not as I know of. But then, they wouldn't put up a sign in their yards to that effect, would they? Listen, Carver, why would a serial killer pick on us old folks? I mean, what'd be the motive?"

That was the question, all right. "Inheritance, maybe," Carver said, hoping he wouldn't have to explain that.

"Rathawk Two, you read me?" the CB radio suddenly blared.

" 'Scuse me," Val told Carver. He unclipped the microphone and held it an inch in front of his mouth. "Rathawk Two here, Louella."

"Woman over on O Street, number five twenty-two, says grandkids visiting next door won't stop playing the stereo too loud. Same songs over and over. Gloria Estefan records are driving her bananas. Wanna check that one out? Over."

Val pressed his mike button. "Ten-four, Louella. Out."

Val clipped the mike back to the dash. "Sometimes we handle that kinda thing," he explained. "Save the police a trip out here when they need to be chasing crooks and crack addicts."

"Logical," Carver said.

"I can drop you back at your car. Another couple bars of Gloria Estefan ain't gonna make much difference."

Carver was a Gloria Estefan fan, but he didn't mention that to Val.

When Val had braked the Dodge next to the parked Olds, he said, "You get lonely, come ride with me again. Maybe I'll buy the doughnuts."

"Too much cholesterol," Carver said. "Bad for the heart."

"Like Russian metal," Val said, depressing the clutch and jamming the gearshift lever into low.

"Russian metal" was the irradiated material KGB espionage agents used to induce seemingly natural death in their victims.

As he watched the Dodge round the corner at a leisurely pace to respond to the audio assault call on O Street, Carver wondered where Rathawk Two had learned such a thing.

| 10 |

CARVER KNEW he'd be dealing with a medical doctor, and he wasn't being operated on, so after breakfast the next morning at the Seagrill Cafe, he sipped coffee until almost ten o'clock before driving over to the medical center.

The same pleasant redhead was at the fourth-floor reception-ist's desk, but she didn't seem to recognize Carver. Dr. Wynn was in, she told him, and like yesterday she invited him to have a seat and wait.

He settled down on a hard little sofa for what he figured would be a long time, resting his cane against one of the cush-ions. From hidden speakers, an FM station that boasted of playing "soft rock" sent out waves of neutered sound from the sixties. It was cool in here, anyway. He might as well relax and listen to violins play Jefferson Airplane.

Only seconds after he'd turned the first page of a tattered two-month-old *Newsweek*, he was aware of someone standing near him.

He looked up and saw a fortyish woman who surely at some

point in her life had won a beauty contest. Her white uniform couldn't mute the effect of her long, shapely legs, lean waist, high and full breasts. Shoulder-length, artfully tousled auburn hair framed a face with high cheekbones, luminous gray eyes, and a narrow, perfect nose. The only break in the symmetry was a slight overbite and pouty lower lip, but that only added to her appeal. It was a mouth made for uninhibited love.

She knew why he was staring at her and smiled, used to men's eyes and what went on behind them. "Mr. Carver?"

He nodded and laid down the *Newsweek*.

"If you'll follow me, I'll lead you to Dr. Wynn's office."

She'd noticed his cane without seeming to, and she walked ahead of him at a slower than normal pace so he could keep up. He didn't mind limping behind her.

She knocked twice perfunctorily on a closed oak door that had a brass DR. ARTHUR WYNN plaque on it, then opened the door and ushered Carver inside.

Carver was in a large, well-furnished office. Soft green leather furniture on a deep brown carpet. Paneled walls adorned with framed diplomas and certificates. In a corner stood a waist-high piece of modern sculpture that appeared to have been fashioned from scores of gleaming steel surgical instruments welded together. Carver wondered what it was called.

The door closed behind Carver, leaving him alone with an athletically built man about fifty who stood up behind his wide desk. He was six feet tall and wore pleated blue pinstripe slacks, a white shirt, red tie, and red and white suspenders, only he probably called them braces. On a corner of the desk was one of those little gadgets with half a dozen suspended steel balls that clicked against each other and maintained seemingly perpetual motion. They were still now.

Dr. Wynn introduced himself and shook Carver's hand, inviting him to sit down in a small upholstered chair with dark wood that matched the desk.

Carver sat. Wynn seemed oblivious of the cane.

"I'm told you're asking some questions on behalf of Jerome Evans's widow," the doctor said. He was tanned as well as fit, with blandly handsome features and razor-styled blond hair that would look white in a certain light. He had large, direct blue eyes, perfect teeth. He might have been a devout surfer who'd become serious between waves and gone into medicine.

"And I'm told you signed the death certificate," Carver said.

Dr. Wynn nodded. "I looked in on the postmortem, then confirmed my conclusions by reading the examining physician's report. More or less standard procedure here, Mr. Carver."

"And you saw nothing unusual in the manner of Jerome's death?"

"Of course not. It was a classic massive coronary. It would have dropped a bull moose dead in its tracks." He swiveled in his chair and gazed out the window at some tall palm trees near the entrance of the parking lot. Swiveled back. "I sympathize with your client, Mr. Carver, I really do. But Hattie Evans isn't the first surviving spouse to question a seemingly untimely death of a partner. This happens for a variety of reasons, from guilt to fear to loneliness. I've seen it before and I'll see it again."

"She said her husband had recently passed a physical."

"At Jerome Evans's stage of life, physical examinations aren't passed or failed, like in the military."

"But neither turned up anything wrong with his heart."

"That's true, and each examination included cholesterol count and an electrocardiogram. Everything seemed normal, so Dr. Billingsly quite correctly didn't go further."

"Further how?"

"Angiogram, CAT scan, various other tests if there's historical or physical indication of heart trouble." Dr. Wynn sank his perfect teeth into his lower lip and was silent for a moment, sitting there handsome, bland, and flawlessly groomed, the quintessential vice-presidential candidate. Then he said, "If Dr.

Billingsly had asked him to undergo these tests, we might well have detected the blood clot that later changed position and killed him. But there was no apparant reason to extend testing. He fooled us, Mr. Carver. Unfortunately, it won't be the last time we'll be fooled, but we try to keep the percentages as low as possible."

"Speaking of percentages," Carver said, "I'm told the death rate in Solartown is somewhat higher than at similar retirement communities." He gave the doctor the figures Beth had recited on the phone.

"A statistical fluke," Dr. Wynn said, "assuming those figures are correct. There's simply no reason why the death rate here should exceed the average, and I'm positive that over a sufficient period of time the numbers will even out."

"If the figures *are* accurate and not a fluke," Carver said, "could you think of any possible explanation?"

The doctor made a steeple with his manicured pink fingers and smiled. "Could you?"

"Something in the water, maybe," Carver said.

The pink steeple contracted and expanded as Dr. Wynn flexed his fingers. "You're joking, but that sort of thing actually happens. So for the record, the Solartown water supply is period-ically checked, carefully monitored." He laced his fingers and lowered his hands to the desk, gazing at Carver with a fresh awareness. "Are you suggesting the presence of a mass murderer in Solartown?"

"That sort of thing actually happens, like something in the water," Carver said. "But I'm not suggesting anything."

"I suppose if that kind of aberration were present, we here at the medical center would be in a position to see signs of it. As far as I know, there are no such signs."

"Except for the statistics I just quoted."

"I can promise you, Mr. Carver, I'll personally check your numbers, and if they're accurate I'll do further research to confirm they can be dismissed as a meaningless statistical blip. Numbers occasionally lie. Despite the polls, Truman defeated Dewey for the presidency."

"Only once," Carver said.

"In the year the Cleveland Indians uncharacteristically won the World Series," Dr. Wynn pointed out.

He had Carver there.

Carver thanked the doctor for his time, stood up, then limped to the door. As soon as his hand touched the knob, the door swung open, held by the smiling beauty who'd escorted him into the office. The lucky name tag on her left breast said she was Monica Gorham, R.N.

"I'll show you out, Mr. Carver," she said in a voice suitable for 900 numbers.

This time she walked beside him in the wide hall.

"Did your talk with Dr. Wynn go well?" she asked.

"Well enough."

"I suppose you wanted to ask him about Jerome Evans."

"What makes you think so?" Carver asked.

"You were here yesterday, making inquiries. It just seemed natural you'd want to see Dr. Wynn. I hope he reassured you."

"He's a reassuring sort," Carver said noncommittally.

"He's a superb administrator," Nurse Gorham said.

"What do you do here?" Carver asked.

"My title is executive director of nursing."

"Head nurse?"

She smiled. "Sometimes much more than that."

It was odd that the executive director of nursing had ushered him into Wynn's office in the manner of a secretary. Maybe she'd wanted to get a close look at Carver, size him up.

They'd reached the elevator. Carver punched the DOWN button with the tip of his cane and said, "Do you have any personal opinions about Jerome Evans, Nurse Gorham?"

"I wouldn't be in a position to form opinions," she said. "I can tell you this, though: Mrs. Evans isn't the first widow to get suspicious in her grief. Even though I wasn't in the O.R. at the time, I know that no one shot or stabbed her husband. This isn't a big-city trauma center, Mr. Carver. We deal with old people, and they die at a faster rate than the young. And very often they go swiftly and unexpectedly, like Jerome Evans."

"Exactly like?"

"Exactly."

A young, heavyset woman in a nurse's uniform was ambling down the hall. She saw Nurse Gorham and immediately picked up her pace. For an instant the kind of hate that can only be generated by fear was in her eyes.

Carver waited until the young nurse had hurried past.

"What about Maude Crane?" he asked.

Nurse Gorham seemed puzzled. "It's a name I don't know."

"It was on the news. She's a Solartown resident who committed suicide the other day."

"I don't have time to keep up with the news, Mr. Carver."

"Maude and Jerome Evans were not-so-secret lovers."

She began to answer, but the elevator arrived and he thanked her and limped inside, leaving her standing there with her mouth open. On any other woman it wouldn't have been attractive.

As the elevator dropped, he wondered why she was more interested than she should be about his talk with Dr. Wynn.

11

THE TEMPERATURE was over ninety by the time Carver got back to the Warm Sands Motel. As he parked the Olds, he noticed the little artificial beach down by the lake was crowded, and there were about a dozen preteen children splashing around in the swimming pool while their parents watched.

Heat from the pavement radiated through the thin soles of his moccasins as he limped to his room. He was perspiring by the time he closed the door behind him.

It felt cool in the room. The drapes were still closed, muffling the voices of the kids in the pool. His grip was slippery with perspiration on the crook of his cane, and his shirt was still plastered to his back from sitting in the car. He made his way into the bathroom, leaned over the washbasin, and ran cold water. After splashing some on his face, he held his wrists beneath the cool stream that twisted shimmering from spigot to drain. He felt better when he limped back into the room.

Until he saw someone standing near the bed.

Carver stood still, tightening his hold on the cane. He knew how to use it as a weapon.

"Startle you?" the man by the bed asked. He was conservatively dressed in a gray suit, white shirt, dark tie with diagonal stripes. His straight, dark hair was short and neatly combed with a part on the side, and he had the kind of clean-shaven, squarish face that prompted the description "clean cut." His eyes were calm behind black horn-rimmed glasses that lent him a bookish air. The well-tailored suit was a fooler; Carver noticed that beneath the slimming effect of artfully draped material, the man's shoulders, chest, and arms were immense.

"I'm not used to walking out of the bathroom and finding Clark Kent," Carver said.

The man smiled. He might have been the muscular host of a TV game show, approving of Carver's cleverness. Or maybe he'd been told before he'd make a great Clark Kent and knew he was really Superman.

"How'd you get in?" Carver asked.

The big man nodded toward the door. "I simply applied pressure. Anyone watching outside would think the door was unlocked and I just walked in."

Carver stared at the sprung latch. He hadn't heard the lock give over the running water in the bathroom with the door closed. It must have taken phenomenal strength to force entry into the room. Superman for sure.

"There must be a reason for your visit," Carver said.

The big man crossed his arms, straining good tropical-blend wool. His hands were large, with thick, blunt fingers and squared-off, clean nails. He wasn't sweating despite the suit coat and tie. He said, "I'll get to the point, which is that I'm here to discourage you from continuing with the Jerome Evans investigation."

"If you're here," Carver said, "there must be something to investigate."

"Obviously."

"Which means I'll only be encouraged to continue."

"Oh, not at all. The fact that my presence suggests information beyond your present knowledge does provide incentive, but that will be far outweighed by the conversation we're about to have."

"What kind of conversation?"

"Animated," the man said.

He stepped toward Carver, moving smoothly for all his bulk. There was no doubt what he had in mind.

Therapeutic swimming, and the very act of locomoting with the cane, had given Carver a powerful upper body. He thought he could handle this guy, even without kryptonite.

But then, that was just the way he thought.

He waited, perfectly still, so he'd surprise the big man all the more with his sudden motion. The distance between them was closing.

Carver swiftly raised the cane and rammed its tip into the man's sternum, inches beneath the heart. He was skilled in using the cane as a jabbing weapon, and he'd taken down some strong men that way. This time his assailant simply grunted softly and brushed the cane aside, more a comment than an expression of pain.

Striking quickly so he wouldn't lose his balance, Carver faked another jab, then lashed out with the cane at the man's head. A huge hand darted out and snatched away the cane before it could make contact.

Carver felt a cold panic as he tottered and started to fall.

But he didn't fall. The big man shoved him back against the wall, supporting him in a standing position. With the speed of a top heavyweight boxer, he slammed a mammoth fist into Carver's stomach. As Carver's breath *whoosh*ed out of him and his mouth gaped, the man inserted the cane and pushed it until its tip pressed against the back of his throat. Carver leaned back tight against the wall, feeling the rough plaster against the back of his head, struggling not to gag.

The big man moved in closer. Carver lifted his good leg to try to knee him in the groin, but the man easily blocked it with his own leg and applied pressure with the cane. Carver choked for several seconds. His stomach, aching from the blow he'd received, went into spasms and he almost vomited.

Smiling confidently, the big man waited until Carver had control of himself, holding the cane steadily, keeping Carver pinned to the wall.

"You might notice," he said, still smiling at Carver but now with a mesmerized expression, "that this will be a sort of one-way conversation. Tough enough for you just to breathe, I'm sure, so I won't ask you to talk."

Carver swung his right fist out at the man's stomach. It was like hitting stucco, and the momentum of the swing pulled him out from the wall. The cane rammed against his tonsils. More choking.

"Keep trying that kind of thing and you'll start to bleed in there, drown on your own blood. I've seen it happen. It's fun to watch."

Saliva was building around the cane, and there *was* the taste of blood. Carver swallowed. It hurt like hell, and he almost went into another choking fit.

That seemed to amuse the man. He was getting his jollies, all right, which infuriated Carver. "We can agree now, I'm sure, that my warning to you to stop your investigation carries some persuasiveness. So, I'm asking you at this point if you intend to be reasonable and apply your talents elsewhere. Do you?"

Carver tried to speak but only gagged. He found himself biting the cane.

"Try to manage a nod," the man said. "That'll be easier."

Carver managed. He felt saliva trickle down his chin.

Another dreamy yet alert smile. The cane rotated painfully between Carver's teeth and against the back of his throat, like a blunt drill bit. "Is that your solemn promise, Mr. Carver?"

It was harder to nod agreement this time, more agonizing.

The man slowly withdrew the cane from Carver's mouth, pressing a forefinger against his own lips in a signal for silence. Then, without a change of expression, he jabbed the tip of the cane into Carver's sternum, exactly as Carver had done to him.

The effect was different. Carver bounced off the wall and lost consciousness for a few seconds. He was on the floor, in the fetal position except for his stiff leg, listening to his harsh rasping struggle for breath and life.

"Gets rough now," the man said.

The cane lashed out, over and over, against the meaty part of Carver's shoulders and upper arms, so quickly he couldn't ward it off. He tucked in his chin and covered his head with his arms, but that didn't matter; his head wasn't the target. Pain exploded through him with each impact, numbing his upper body. He could actually hear the whir of the cane each time it descended, but it didn't allow time for him to brace for the blow.

Breathing only slightly harder, the big man finally stepped back.

"I aim to convince," he said. He adjusted his black horn-rims with his little finger, in a way that was almost prissy. Then he raised his left arm as if about to check his wristwatch. Instead he lashed out at his own tensed forearm with such strength and swiftness that the hard walnut cane splintered across it.

He casually tossed the ruined cane onto the carpet, next to Carver, and said, "Convinced?"

Carver nodded, trying not to vomit or lose consciousness. Bile lay bitter in his throat. His good leg was curled up tight against his stomach.

"You can talk now," the man said, deftly adjusting his glasses again on the bridge of his nose.

Carver tried to say he was convinced. It was agree or die; he was sure of it. Only an inarticulate croaking came out. He was terrified his answer might be misinterpreted.

But apparently his attacker understood. Or at least was satisfied with the effort. He very deliberately and gently prodded Carver with the toe of his shoe. Then he brushed his hands together as if whisking dust from his palms, adjusted his tie knot, and nodded good-bye. His appearance and attitude was that of a salesman who'd just completed a successful office call.

Sunlight angled across the carpet, then disappeared, as the door opened and closed. Children's shouts from pool and beach, which had entered the room with the outside glare, were abruptly cut off.

It was suddenly very quiet. Dim. Cool.

Carver lay with his cheek pressed against the coarse carpet, still in the fetal position but for his protruding stiff leg. He surrendered and let himself plunge with increasing speed through blackness to a place where there was no pain.

WHEN HE awoke he was lying on his back on the bed and he was sweating. His shoes had been removed. The back of his throat felt as if it had been sandpapered, and his stomach ached as if he'd eaten a hundred green apples. When he tried to lift his hand from the mattress to wipe his forehead, he discovered with a sledgehammer smash of pain that his entire upper body was stiff and sore, as if he'd been in a serious auto accident.

Someone groaned. Must have been him.

The mattress shifted and bedsprings sang. A cool, soft hand rested against his forehead. Familiar hand.

Beth said, "Who did this to you, Fred?"

"He didn't leave his card," Carver said hoarsely. At least he could still speak.

"One man?"

He nodded.

"Lord!"

Sitting on the edge of the mattress, she stared down at him with her own pain and concern. She was wearing faded Levi's, a yellow sleeveless blouse, and a headband with a daisy design on it. She looked like an African princess dressed down for the occasion. "I'm gonna call a doctor."

"Don't do that. I don't want anybody from the medical center." God, it hurt to talk!

"Then I'm gonna drive you into Orlando. Get you goddamn looked at, and I don't want any argument."

"Not yet."

She stood up from the bed. "Not yet my ass!"

"Let me stay here awhile. I'm feeling better, believe it or not."

"Not," she said. But she made no move to pry him from the bed. She cursed under her breath. "Feeling well enough to tell me what happened?"

"Slowly," he said.

She sat back down on the bed, her hip warm against his side. "Slow as you want. Then we're going to see a doctor."

And he told her.

"THE CANE as phallic symbol," she said, when he was finished.

"If that's the case, it coulda been worse."

"Maybe it will be next time. You better take this scumbag seriously."

He was surprised by the fear in her voice, the rage in her dark eyes. He said, "I take him seriously, all right."

She stood up and took a few hurried steps this way and that. Tall, elegant woman. "Shit, Fred! You need to back off this one."

He said nothing. His own rage was building. He did feel as if somehow he'd been intimately violated, symbolic oral sex. For a moment an insight: Did rape victims feel this way? His hate for the man in the horn-rimmed glasses took root deep in him, hard and fast, the craving for revenge.

"Fred?"

"I'm thinking."

"Bet you're not. Bet you're feeling."

"Feeling lousy," he said.

He moved to struggle to a sitting position, reaching for his cane with a stab of pain. Then he remembered the casual destruction of the cane after it had been used to beat him. It had been a skillful beating, bruising but not breaking, and he was reasonably sure there was no long-term injury. He was also sure the man who'd assaulted him was a professional thug. In the unlikely event of an arrest, by the time the victim of such a beating made it into a courtroom, the bruises would have long since faded. Prosecutors were left to try to prove that photographs, if there were any, weren't images of faked injuries.

Beth worked an arm beneath one of his and lifted gently, but it still caused a jolt of pain and he ground his teeth.

"You oughta see," she said. "You got welts all over you. You oughta fucking see!"

"I don't have to see to know they're there. I don't have my cane."

"I know, lover. I'll help you out to the car."

He leaned on her strong, lithe body, taking it slow, making it to the door with its useless locks. Have to make repairs.

Outside, he squinted against the glare, and the heat hit him like a falling wall. A few people by the pool stopped what they were doing and stared as Beth helped ease him into the passenger side of her LeBaron convertible. A small, shapely woman in a red bathing suit slung a towel across her shoulders and gazed openly with her head cocked to the side. He leaned back in the seat and closed his eyes to the brilliance and heat of the sun.

Great! Beth had the car's top down. That was why she wore the flowered sweatband, to keep her hair from flying in her face.

Quickly, she started the engine, raised the canvas top, and switched on the air conditioner.

Then she drove fast and artfully, leaning forward to peer through the windshield intensely and gripping the steering wheel with both hands in the ten-and-two-o'clock position. On turns, she shuffled the steering wheel through her hands instead of crossing her arms. Knew her stuff. Maybe she'd driven get-away while living with her drug-czar husband. Wheel moll, if there was such a thing.

Unfair of him to think that, Carver decided. He wasn't one to muck around in the past, anyway. It made no difference to him what she'd done in that phase of her life; being judgmental was a game he didn't play. Who was he, Albert Schweitzer?

The car's interior had barely cooled down when she swerved into a circular driveway, then parked by the tinted glass doors of a hospital emergency entrance.

|12|

A NURSE placed cold compresses on Carver's arms and shoulders to contain the swelling, while a young doctor whose name was Doris Loa swabbed his throat with disinfectant.

"This is about all we can do for you, Mr. Carver," Dr. Loa told him, still with the cotton swab pressed against his tonsils. Apparently she didn't expect an answer. She was a dark-complexioned, dark-eyed woman of about thirty with Asiatic features and an air of calm competence.

Finally she removed the swab, leaving him with a stinging sensation at the back of his throat and a persistent taste of iodine. She stepped back, dropped the used swab into a plastic-lined receptacle, and said, "How'd this happen?"

"Accident," Carver said, before Beth could speak.

"That right?" She looked at Beth, who shrugged and nodded simultaneously. "Fell down some stairs, I bet," Dr. Loa said.

"Fifteen steps," Carver said. "Loose throw rug. Dangerous. When's this bitter taste gonna go away?"

"Soon. What about the throat?"

"I was eating a Popsicle when I fell."

"Those damned wooden sticks," Dr. Loa said. She smiled hopelessly; she went from plain to attractive when she smiled. "I'm too busy to pry. I'm going to write you a prescription for pain pills and an antibiotic to reduce the possibility of infection. Call me if there are any complications. And I mean *any*." A meaningful glance at Beth, conspiracy between the sexes. "Make sure that he does call."

"You can see he's easy to influence," Beth said.

"I picked up on that. But I don't want to treat him in the future for something more serious, if whoever beat him up with a throw rug, stairs, and Popsicle decides to get meaner."

"Now I feel like a real patient," Carver said, "being talked about as if I'm not here."

"Or as if you hadn't followed doctor's orders and you died," Dr. Loa told him. She parted pale-green curtains and was gone before Carver could say anything.

"Woman knows how to make a point," Beth said.

On the way out of the hospital, they stopped at the prescription counter at the end of the hall and picked up the antibiotic and Percodan pain pills. Carver also bought a replacement cane. There was a spare cane in the trunk of the Olds, back at the motel, but the way things were going, it wasn't a bad idea to keep his supply at two.

"What now?" Beth asked, as they walked across the hot parking lot to where she'd moved the car. There were dark clouds stacked on the horizon, and the humidity was trying hard to keep up with the temperature.

"We're going to police headquarters."

She broke stride, surprised. "You gonna report this? File a complaint?"

"Not exactly. I need to talk to Desoto."

Beth snorted. "Oughta let him know he's the one got you into this." She liked Desoto, but despite his attraction to and for women, he'd never fully accepted her as a positive aspect of Carver's life. He was a cop, and he couldn't quite get around her background. Beth claimed not to be bothered by Desoto's polite coolness, but Carver didn't believe her. She said, "You'd be better off if you rested awhile back at the motel, then drove in to talk to Desoto later."

"I don't wanna waste time."

"Such an obsessive bastard," Beth said, unlocking the car door, then climbing in to reach across and unlock the opposite door for Carver.

"Can't you think of me as determined?" he asked, after he'd lowered himself into the passenger seat. His arms and shoulders were still plenty sore, but the cold compresses had made the pain tolerable.

"The difference between determined and obsessive is a fine line," she told him. "You're way across it and on the other side, lover."

He was irritated. She was merciless, to pick on him when he was sitting here aching everywhere from the waist up. "You think I'm obsessive, why do you stay with me?"

"It's why I love you, Fred. Let's stop someplace and get some ice cream 'fore we go see Desoto. It'll be my lunch, and it'll make that sore throat of yours feel better."

Carver thought that was a sound idea. Numb his throat and get rid of the taste of iodine. Not that he was hungry.

She started the car, switched the air conditioner on high, and shifted to reverse. Both hands on the steering wheel, ready to drive, she looked over at him. "Ice cream?"

He nodded.

She grinned. "You glad I came, Fred?"

He wasn't sure. Didn't answer.

AFTER DOUBLE scoops at a frozen yogurt place on Orange Avenue, Beth drove the few blocks to police headquarters and parked on a side street off Hughey. Carver had ordered low-fat strawberry, while Beth of the fashion-model figure had spooned down extra-rich French vanilla laced with crumbled Oreo cookies. The chubby teenage girl behind the counter had given her looks colder than the yogurt.

Beth didn't like police stations, she told Carver, any more than she liked dietary frozen yogurt. She'd take a walk while he was inside seeing Desoto, then meet him in about half an hour at the car.

"Might take more'n half an hour," Carver said.

"Then I'll take another walk. Maybe get another couple scoops of cookies and yogurt. Ruin my shape."

He had to smile. "Don't roam too far away," he said. He climbed out of the car, waited a few seconds, then limped across Hughey when there was a break in the traffic.

The desk sergeant said Desoto was in a meeting, so Carver sat on a long wooden bench and watched people come and go. Plainclothes detectives with their loose-jointed, too-casual air. Uniforms swaggering with their arms swinging out from their bodies to avoid the gear strapped to their belts. A down-and-out old man who looked like a street person, being booked for loitering, but not understanding. Bewildered, as if old age and destitution had caught up with him overnight. He kept widening his eyes and asking about a lottery, apparently thinking he'd won something. The desk sergeant was getting exasperated. The young uniform who'd brought in the loiterer looked alternately sad and amused, learning about life's puzzle.

When the old guy had finally been booked and taken to a holdover cell, the phone rang, and the desk sergeant held it to his ear briefly then hung up and told Carver he could go back to Desoto's office.

A couple of plainclothes cops nodded to Carver as he limped along the hall, remembering him from his department days. They'd all been in uniform then.

Desoto was hanging up his cream-colored suit coat when Carver entered through the open door. There was an ornate brass hook on the wall near his desk, where he often hung his coats. Only he never put them directly on the hook, always used a shaped wooden hanger.

"*Amigo,*" he said, nodding a hello to Carver and sitting down behind his desk as Carver sat. He was wearing a white-on-white shirt with gold cuff links and a gold tie bar, flowered tie with a lot of yellow in it, tan leather shoulder holster. The well-dressed cop's ensemble. Did Desoto have a different color gun for each outfit? "You're moving a bit gingerly today." He didn't seem to have noticed that about Carver, but he had.

Carver told him why he was moving gingerly.

"So," Desoto said, when he was finished, "you want to file a complaint?"

"Maybe to complain that filing a complaint wouldn't do any good."

"Yeah, we both know how it works. The guy who did a job on you has probably got an alibi and two backup alibis."

Carver said he knew. "What I want is to find out who he is."

"Oh, I just bet you do. You wanna let him finish what he started." Desoto shook his handsome head. His sleek black hair didn't budge. "You latch onto something like this, you make a pit bull seem like a quitter."

Carver hoped he wasn't going to start in with that "obsessive" talk again. Like Beth on the drive over. There was too much psychoanalysis in the world; things were complicated enough without it. Therapy had its uses, but it had also become the narcotic of the law-abiding. Can't cope? No need to learn. See an expert. Again and again and again. People were taking therapists like Valium.

"Commitment to revenge can be your fuel, *amigo*, and it can also get you killed."

"It isn't only revenge," Carver told him. "If somebody wants me to turn loose of the Jerome Evans investigation, it's because there must be something to investigate."

"That hadn't escaped me," Desoto said. "But it won't make you any less dead."

"Beth's waiting for me outside," Carver said. "Why don't you feed the tough guy's description into the process while I examine mug shots?"

"How come she didn't come in with you?"

"I think you make her nervous."

Desoto didn't say anything. Then he stood up. "Can you walk okay?"

Carver said he could. He stood up and leaned hard on the cane.

Desoto led him to a small room not much larger than a storage closet. It contained three chairs and a rectangular oak table. The pale-green walls were grease-stained and badly in need of paint. There were three stacks of thickly bound mug books on the table. The only light was from the single, dust-coated window.

"I'll leave you here to look for the right photo," Desoto said. "While you're doing that, I'll get the description in circulation."

Carver thanked him and settled down on a hard wooden chair, making it a point not to groan with discomfort. By the time he'd dragged the first of the large, heavy books over, Desoto had left and closed the door softly behind him.

Carver was alone in the tiny, quiet room with the sun streaming like a celestial spotlight through the incredibly dirty, wire-reinforced window behind him, illuminating the rogues' gallery in front of him.

As if it were a book of saints.

13

ONLY TWENTY minutes had passed before Desoto came back into the room. He was carrying a yellow file folder and some fanfold computer paper with faint dot-matrix printing on it. Hard copy, Desoto called it these days, now that he'd become computer literate.

"You still on the first book, *amigo*?"

Carver said, "I want to be sure."

"Well, I can save you some trouble, I think. VICAP had a file on your guy. In fact, there's a wealth of information about him. He fascinates people, like a lot of predators do. Name Adam Beed strike a chord?"

Carver closed the mug book and shook his head no.

Desoto drew a fax photo from the folder and laid it on the table. The face of the man who'd attacked Carver stared up at him. Yet as he looked longer at the grainy black-and-white image he couldn't be positive. Desoto laid another photo before Carver; in this one Beed was wearing his black horn-rimmed glasses. No doubt about who it was. He was also wearing the horn-rims in the defiant, chin-up profile shot Desoto placed on the table. He looked more upwardly mobile than criminal.

"Him," Carver said, feeling something warm and fierce growing in his belly.

Desoto sat down across from Carver at the table. He had his suit coat on but he didn't appear to be uncomfortable in the stifling room. "I made some calls, *amigo*, learned plenty about Beed. He was an accountant at a major investment firm, got into trouble with embezzlement six years ago, and did a stretch in Raiford."

Carver stared at him. "An accountant?"

Desoto smiled. "He had your number, hey?"

"How long's he been out?" Carver asked.

"Paroled eighteen months ago. When he was in prison he underwent a kind of metamorphosis. Within a couple of years he was nothing like the soft, white-collar type who walked through the gates. Took to weight training, martial arts, lightened up on cocaine."

"He had a habit?"

"Oh, yes. That was why he embezzled, to support it. He was still on the stuff in prison, but he had to moderate. Despite what the public hears, drugs aren't all that easy to get inside the walls. Not like out here, anyway. Beed got bigger and stronger, then bigger and stronger again. Then he went about getting even with an inmate who'd raped him when he was new, a tough hombre in for murder. Nothing can be proved, but it seems the fella lost his left arm in a workshop accident. Naturally enough, he won't talk about what really happened."

"Maybe Beed broke it off," Carver said.

"A joke, *amigo*?"

"I suppose," Carver said. "I get fed up hearing how tough assholes like Beed are, how they plow over everybody who gets in their way." Outside in the distance a siren warbled frantically, maybe responding to a call about a crime perpetrated by one of the world's Adam Beeds. Carver hated the takers in life. Right now, Beed in particular. "Get on with your story," he said.

Desoto said, "Beed became a sadistic homosexual himself, and rumor has it he murdered his cellmate. Again, nothing provable. Beed can put on an act in front of investigators or a parole board. And he still thinks and acts like an accountant. He's conservative in dress and manner, the kind of guy you'd trust in a minute to date your daughter or keep your books."

"Your daughter and books," Carver said, "not mine. If Beed's on parole, you must have a current address on him."

Desoto laughed. "No, my friend. You aren't hearing what I'm saying about this one. He's different. This kind of animal breaks parole the first week he's released, then disappears. It's predictable, and that's what happened with Beed. But like I said, he's cautious. He knew he'd lose big if he got nailed for possession of illegal narcotics in prison, so the word is he replaced his cocaine habit with alcohol dependency. Not his drug of choice, but he had to make do if he didn't want a lot of years behind bars."

"Is that all that's on his sheet?" Carver asked. "The embezzlement conviction?"

"That's it, *amigo*. I told you he was different. I said it's suspected he killed his cellmate, but I didn't talk about method. The cellmate was a little guy named Kravak, in for a homicide committed while he was burglarizing a drugstore. Prison guards found Kravak dead; he'd been tortured with lighted cigarettes touched to the bottoms of his feet, his genitals, eyelids, everywhere. Took the prison doctors a while to figure out what killed him, though. A straightened wire coat hanger inserted through his rectum. It pierced everything right up to and including his heart."

Carver pushed away his revulsion and replaced it with resolve. Some of his fear he left intact; he'd need it to keep an edge, to avoid making a dumb move based on emotion. "So Beed's an unreserved sadist. You think I don't know that?"

Desoto's somber brown eyes were steady. He meshed his fingers, gold rings flashing in the blast of sunlight through the window. "Something else, *amigo*. They found the cellmate in a storeroom, and in the condition I just described. But also, there were bites out of him."

Carver felt his stomach pulse against his belt buckle. "Jesus! We talking cannibalism?"

"Probably not. More like old-fashioned cruelty with a disgusting twist. It took the doctors a few days to realize they were looking at bites; things had been done to the wounds with a knife so it'd be impossible to match tooth patterns."

Carver sat back and watched dust motes swirl in the angled shaft of sunlight bisecting the room. The siren had faded to silence outside. Maybe the bad guy was caught, and a modicum of order had been restored to the world.

"This Beed," Desoto said, "he's strong as an Olympic weight lifter, and he's a psycho. He was a monster in prison, and I was told he's been taking steroids since his release, maybe even was on them behind the walls, so he's even more dangerous."

Carver was getting weary of the buildup. And angry. "The man's not a goddamn tank."

"No, he's much more dangerous. He's got a brain, he's more maneuverable than a tank, and meaner. Follow his advice, *amigo*. Give your apologies to Hattie Evans. Say your good-byes and continue to live."

"And the law will take over the case?"

Desoto shrugged with elegant sadness. "There are no witnesses to Beed's attack on you, and as I said, he would have an alibi even if we did manage to locate him and pick him up for violating parole. So there still isn't enough to warrant an official investigation of Jerome Evans's death. If it were up to me, maybe, but I have to answer to the higher-ups. That's why I sent Hattie to you, hey?"

"And now you're telling me to turn her away."

"Yes. You can't bring her husband back to life, which is what she really wants. Instead you'll join him in death. I know how you think, *amigo*, how you get fixated."

"It's my job to get fixated. That's the kind of game we're in and you know it."

"Maybe that's how you think of it, like some kind of game. That I understand. But this Beed is much more than an opponent; he's a force. You should hope he goes somewhere else to cause problems. Or you could wait until a bullet from his dangerous world claims him."

"But you know he won't go somewhere else," Carver said, shifting his weight over his cane and standing up. "And there's no way to predict the where or when of bullets."

Desoto stood also, buttoning and smoothing his suit coat. "Which is why you should go back to Del Moray and tend to other business."

He seemed to be waiting for Carver to agree. Hoping.

"Thanks for this," Carver said, limping toward the door.

"*Amigo*, you gonna smarten up and quit this thing? I mean, I'm in a way responsible for what might happen."

"I'll think about it," Carver said. He reached the door and opened it, waiting for Desoto to catch up.

But when he looked around he saw Desoto leaning back against the table with his arms crossed, his ankles crossed, losing the crease of his expensive slacks. He was gazing at Carver with infinite sadness.

He said, "You lied to me, my friend, when you said you'd think about quitting. Am I right?"

"No. I'll think about it. Anybody would."

"But you won't quit."

"Probably not."

"Would it kill you to quit?"

"Part of me."

"Isn't that better than all of you dying?"

"No."

"Hmph!"

Carver supported himself with a hand on the doorknob, passing the tip of his cane back and forth over the floor in a compact, sweeping motion. Desoto knew why he'd come here. Knew what he'd do with the information. Now, because the information was more volatile than he'd imagined, he was pressuring. The way higher-ups in the department pressured him. He should understand that.

Carver said, "They ever find that arm?"

Desoto didn't smile, but then Carver hadn't expected him to.

He limped from the room.

Behind him, Desoto said softly, "Then stay in touch. Stay alive."

14

BETH HAD figured the time right and was leaning on the LeBaron when Carver crossed Hughey. The late-afternoon sun highlighted her bold features, prominent cheekbones, elegant sinewy neck and arms. She looked like an *Ebony* model posing for a car ad. Her score was perfect; every passing male motorist did a double take.

Carver leaned on his cane in the heat and brilliance that she seemed to radiate and said, "You're liable to cause a traffic accident."

She said, "It's happened before."

They got in the car and she started the engine, switched on the air conditioner, but didn't drive away. "Get what you wanted in there, Fred?"

He sat back and let cool air from the vents flow over him like water. "Yes and no."

"What'd Desoto have to say?"

"He tried hard to impress upon me what a bad boy Adam Beed is."

"Beed the guy did the job on you?"

"Uh-huh."

"So where's that leave you?"

"Trying to impress upon *you* what a bad boy Beed is." He told her what Desoto had said about Adam Beed, watching her profile as he spoke. His words didn't seem to be making an impact. Nothing in her expression changed; she'd heard a lot, seen a lot, long before she'd met Carver.

"Some of this isn't new to me," she said when he'd finished. "I heard of Beed when I was with Roberto. He's different for sure. You oughta be scared of him, Fred."

Carver felt something in his gut tense. Muscle working on dread. "Beed know who you are?"

"No, he was making his reputation in Raiford, and Roberto was dead by the time he got out. He insulted a man who used to work for Roberto. Roberto passed the word and had one of his thugs behind walls work over Beed. About six months later, the man lost an arm. Roberto knew Beed was responsible and tried to have him killed, but Beed had changed in some spooky way and even the worst of the other inmates wouldn't mess with him. Roberto kept track of him, learned more about him, and decided to leave him alone." She turned her head to look straight at Carver for a moment. "Roberto never did that with anyone else. Never even considered it."

Carver knew what she meant. Roberto Gomez had been vicious in the manner of big-time drug dealers who'd achieved success the hard way, and it was a point of honor and good business to make people pay for even the slightest affront. Once he'd set out to teach Beed a lesson, it had cost him plenty to back off. Yet he had. Beed must be something.

"You even a little bit considering walking away from this, Fred?"

"No."

"I was afraid of that."

"What about you going back to Del Moray?"

"I think not," she said. She drummed long, red-enameled fingernails on the steering wheel, watching the traffic on Hughey streaking away from them. "What now? We gonna try to convince each other?"

He thought about it. "No," he said. "You're too stubborn. Here's how we play it. You work under the cover of doing a feature article on Solartown for *Burrow*. That way you can be around, do some probing, and it'll seem unconnected with what I'm doing."

"That's sensible enough, Fred. You think Beed will be watching you?"

"Beed or somebody else."

"We been seen together already."

"I don't think we have by the wrong people. Beed'll give it a few days before checking to see if I heeded his warning. The best thing for him would be if I faded quietly away. He might enjoy trouble, but from what I've heard he's too smart to want it. He'll combine business with pleasure only if there's no other way."

"I expect you're right. Man can't be a fool, more like a mean machine with a brain."

"And if anybody does ask, say we met at the motel and you interviewed me about being a private detective. Always a subject of interest to those who never had to piss in a bottle on stakeout."

"One hitch, here. I'm supposed to keep on with the interview while we're sleeping together?"

"Won't come up," Carver said. "Register at the Warm Sands, so we can get together easily and talk, but we won't share a room."

She put the car in drive and pulled away from the curb, cutting off someone who reacted with a long, angry blast of the horn. She seemed not to hear. "Just what I always wanted to be, a celibate spy."

"Best kind," Carver said. "Can't be blackmailed."

"Until one night."

"Drop me off by my car before you register at the motel," Carver said. "I'm gonna go see Hattie and find out if Jerome Evans and Adam Beed might have been connected in any way."

She drove silently for a few minutes. Then she said, "Since it'd be safer if you found Beed rather than vice versa, I can put out the word with some of my old contacts in the drug business, maybe learn where he can be found these days. He wouldn't have to know who's doing the asking."

"I thought of that," Carver said. "It can't be a hundred percent safe. I'll find Beed on my own. He's on alcohol now, anyway, not part of the illegal drug scene."

"That's a maybe. If he was doing heroin or crack in a major way, alcohol'd only be so much water to him."

"Solartown information's all I want from you," Carver said. "Or all I want that it's smart for you to give." He realized he was pressing the tip of his cane into the car's floor, feeling road and engine vibration running through the shaft. "You'll be safest if you're simply a journalist who happens to be staying at the Warm Sands."

"Want it or not," she told him, "there's something else I'm gonna do for you. I'm gonna drive into Del Moray and bring back your gun."

He considered trying to talk her out of that, then thought about Adam Beed and said nothing.

He settled back in the vinyl upholstery, closed his eyes, and let his bruises heal.

15

THIS TIME Carver refused lemonade, then sat down across from Hattie in her quiet living room. He was in an upholstered chair with dark wood arms. She was perched primly on the edge of the cream-colored sofa. On a table not far from the door, a tall cut-glass vase held half a dozen roses. In the bowels of the house a blower clicked on. Cool air began to whisper through the vents.

"Did Jerome ever mention a man named Adam Beed?" Carver asked. He laid his cane across his lap to avoid leaving a circular depression in the deep carpet. He'd been told about that.

Hattie gazed off to the side, thinking. She said, "No, I'm sure he never mentioned the name." She peered more closely at Carver. "Are those bruises on your arms?" Her tone of voice suggested he'd been fighting in the cloakroom and would be kept after class.

"They are," Carver confirmed, for some reason feeling guilty.

Hattie hadn't lost her schoolteacher ways; she could strike to vulnerability like a barbed arrow.

"Something to do with Mr. Beed?" she asked.

"I had some trouble with him. You're sure your husband didn't know Beed? He's an accountant."

She smiled. "The sort of accountant I'd like to take with me for a tax audit. But neither Jerome nor I have had any dealings with the man." Her back remained perfectly rigid as she folded her hands in her lap. "Why did he strike you, Mr. Carver?"

"He suggested I stop looking into Jerome's death."

"Ah!" Her shrewd eyes got a faraway look. She'd grasped immediately what that meant. "That means there *must* have been something irregular about what happened to Jerome."

"Means there probably was," Carver said. "Doesn't mean it can be proved."

"Isn't proving it why I hired you?"

"Yes, but I can't manufacture evidence out of suspicion. Though it's been done."

She stood up and began to pace, glancing at him now and then, making him feel he'd better not get caught cheating on an exam. "I'm more determined than ever to get to the bottom of this," she said, "but I think you should take your leave of the case. I don't want to be responsible for anyone getting seriously hurt."

"You can't pursue this yourself," Carver pointed out.

She stopped pacing and faced him squarely. "What about the police? Considering what happened to you, won't they take up the investigation?"

Carver explained to her what Desoto had explained to him, that there wasn't enough concrete evidence to justify diverting manpower for what still was officially a natural death. The war on drugs was the great consumer of police time, especially in Florida.

She sat back down, looking thoughtful. Worried. "You mean they're not interested in a possible homicide if the victim was old and nearing death anyway?"

"No," Carver said, "Desoto doesn't think that way." He didn't tell Hattie that certain of Desoto's superiors might follow that line of reasoning.

She rubbed a finger along her chin. "Nevertheless, they won't investigate."

"I will," Carver said. "Things are getting too interesting for me to quit."

"I can't ask that of you."

"Hattie, you can't get me to stop."

She refolded her hands in her lap and stared at him. "No, I can see that you're not persuadable on that point. But are you continuing down this road for the wrong reasons, Mr. Carver?"

"Right reasons or wrong, the destination is the same."

"If you reach it."

"Someone will be helping me," he said, "but don't mention her. She's Beth Jackson, a tall black woman. She's a journalist doing a piece on Solartown. I'm telling you this only so you'll know who she is if she contacts you."

"I believe I talked to her on the phone," Hattie said. "She seemed a capable woman. I'm assuming knowledge of any connection between you two might place her in danger."

"From Adam Beed," Carver said, "as well as other sources."

"There's no shortage of people here who spread tales. I won't mention her to anyone. Wagging tongues will be no problem."

Carver stood up. "I'll keep you informed."

"Do you need more money, Mr. Carver?"

"Not now. I'll let you know."

"Please do." She smiled sternly at him. "You're making fine progress."

Carver got out of there before she pasted a star on his forehead.

INSTEAD OF going to where the Olds was parked, he hobbled across sunbaked lawn to the house next door. VAL GREEN RESIDENCE was stenciled in green paint on a black mailbox. In the center of the door was a V-shaped brass knocker. Carver punched the doorbell button with his cane. Heard nothing from inside. He used the knocker, three brittle cracks of sound that had to be heard throughout the house.

Still no answer.

Val figured to be home; he'd driven as part of the Posse last night and probably had duty again tonight.

Carver decided maybe he was sleeping and limped down from the porch. He was about to walk down the driveway to his car when he heard a faint popping sound coming from behind the house. Instead of heading for the street, he hobbled over rough ground along the side of the house.

The sound was getting louder. It was now a series of *chonks!* with intervals of a few seconds between each one.

Chonk!

Carver peered around the corner of the house.

Chonk!

He saw a machete flash in the sun. A man with his back to him was chopping something on the ground. Fear slithered through Carver, to the core of him. He wished Beth had returned from Del Moray with his Colt .38 automatic and he had it with him.

The man turned around and wiped his forehead with a red handkerchief.

It was Val.

He saw Carver and grinned, dropping the machete as if commanded to at gunpoint.

As Carver limped toward him he realized what Val was doing. He'd been hacking the bottom fronds from a large palm tree, leaving only the upper branches and creating something that would resemble a giant pineapple. At the base of the tree were the fronds Val had removed, and he'd been chopping them into small sections he could bundle and tie to be hauled away.

"Too hot for that kinda work," Carver said.

"Ain't gonna get much cooler this evening." Val used both hands to twist the red handkerchief tight, then stretched it and tied it around his head as a bandana to catch perspiration. "Besides, I gotta go back on duty at eleven."

"Ever heard of an Adam Beed?" Carver asked, standing there sweating in the sun and wishing he had a bandana.

Val stared at Carver's bruised arms. "He the guy did the heavy work on you?"

Carver nodded, watching a cloud of gnats swarming around Val, who didn't seem to notice them.

"Never heard of Beed, but I'll let you know if I do."

"How about Dr. Wynn, over at the medical center?" Carver asked.

Val shrugged, finally waved a hand at the cloud of gnats. "Oh, I know of him, all right. In charge of the whole shebang. Seems a good doctor, too. Does a fine job running the medical center. Ask me, he's a straight enough sort. And I tell you, Carver, anything you wanna know about folks at the medical center, you just ask, 'cause I did volunteer work over there till about six months ago, when I quit so I could devote more time to the Posse. I know most all of 'em."

"Including Nurse Monica Gorham?"

Val's leprechaun features arced up in a smile. "Hard to leave her out. She's some pumpkin, that one. Head nurse there, and really runs the other nurses. She knows her job medically and administratively. Rumor has it she's involved with one of the doctors, but could be only rumor. Tales go around now and then about her being mixed up in some kind of kinky sex. Even stories about her mistreating some of the patients. But crazy gossip's bound to spring up around a woman looks like Nurse Gorham."

"Ever have any trouble with her?"

"No, we got along okay. But I saw some nurses get their tails chewed royally, and not for much reason. Nurse Gorham says jump, they're already off the ground before they ask how high. Pretty as she is, ain't no doubt she's got a streak of cruelty in her, if you catch my meaning." He sputtered, then spat out a gnat. Made a face and wiped a hand across his mouth. He glanced at the Evans house. "How's Hattie doing?"

"Good enough. She's still determined to find out everything about Jerome's death."

"Can't blame her. She's under one hell of a strain."

"Maybe she should move," Carver said. "Get away from this place and its memories."

Val looked alarmed for a moment, then grinned and shook his head. "She won't move. Can't, really. I happened to learn one day from Jerome that their house was bought on the reverse mortgage arrangement."

"Meaning what?"

"Lotta Solartown residents sell their former homes, pay cash for the Solartown houses, and in effect become lenders to Solartown, Incorporated. Solartown then makes monthly payments to them for the rest of their lives. If for some reason a retiree wants to move, monthly payments stop, and full ownership of the house reverts to Solartown. We retire here because the system allows us to get more of a place for the money, while we allow Solartown to play the odds. Insurance guys figured it all out so Solartown does okay, but it's gotta be a win-win situation for the buyer."

"How so?" Carver asked. He was suspicious of win-win situations. Politicians and confidence artists used the term frequently.

Val said, "So long as the retiree lives in the house, it's a good deal and provides the security of a monthly income. If the retiree dies before the full price of the house is paid out, it's a bad deal, but so what, the owner's dead and it don't matter. There are no really bad deals for the dead, Carver. So, it's win-win for us, and Solartown can't lose in the long run because of the actuarial odds. Works out for most residents, but now and then Solartown reacquires a piece of valuable property that's just been paid for in full within the last few years. So I can tell you they do just fine by the arrangement. Win-win. That make sense?"

"For now it does," Carver said, sensing a scam. Sensing a motive. "Where's the Solartown developer's office?"

"In Orlando, on Orange Avenue. I went there once to sign some papers."

Carver thanked Val and turned to move away.

"Hey there, Carver. You wanna ride patrol with me tonight? You can get an idea of what the Posse does around here."

"I'll take you up on that some other time," Carver said.

"Any night's okay. And remember to call on me if you want any sorta help with what you're doing for Hattie."

"I might take you up on that, too," Carver told him.

"She's a highly exceptional woman and don't deserve all this crap," Val said.

Carver agreed, waving good-bye with his free hand as he limped across the yard toward the street. Sweat was rolling down his back. He could feel dampness around the waistband of his pants. Behind him, Val spat out another gnat.

As Carver lowered himself into the Olds, he heard again the regular *chonk! chonk!* of the machete striking home.

16

CARVER SLEPT until after nine the next morning, late for him. He reached over and felt smooth, cool linen and wished Beth were in the bed with him instead of in a room at the other end of the motel. When he started to sit up, a train smashed into him.

He let himself drop back down onto the mattress, staring straight up at the ceiling. His injured muscles had stiffened, and his bruises were even more painful than they'd been yesterday. He knew it wouldn't be easy to get the old machine moving this morning, but it had to be done. The curse of duty.

This time when he worked himself into a sitting position he thought about Adam Beed. Barely pausing, he groped for and found his cane and levered himself up to stand near the bed.

Ignoring the pain, the sour taste in his mouth, the fact that he was moving like a longtime Solartown resident, he hobbled into the bathroom. He reassured himself with the knowledge that Beed had skillfully not broken anything; he'd wanted Carver fit enough to travel.

For a moment Carver studied himself in the mirror above the washbasin. The bruises marking his arms, chest, and shoulders were deep purple now, sometimes tinged with the ugly red color of ruptured small blood vessels close to the surface of the skin. Beed was good at his work, all right.

After brushing his teeth to get the nasty taste from his mouth, he ran a glass of cold water. He downed a couple of Percodan tablets, then regarded the fool in the mirror and smiled tolerantly. The fool smiled back.

Carver leaned his cane on the washbasin and used the frosted glass doors and a towel rack for support as he twisted the faucet handle and climbed into the shower. He kept his hand on the chrome handle jutting from the gray ceramic tile beneath the shower head and eased the water temperature to as hot as he could endure. Then he stood for a long time beneath the stinging needles of water as billows of steam rose around him to turn the tiny shower stall and bathroom into a sauna.

Forty-five minutes later he was dressed, feeling less pain and stiffness, not ready to rumba, but moving reasonably well. After calling the motel office to have the lock on his door repaired, he got out of the cool room and had a waffle, Canadian bacon, and coffee at the Seagrill, glancing around for Beth while he ate, but not seeing her. Sleeping late, he figured. Or maybe she'd gone down to the artificial beach and lake for a morning swim. He pictured her in her skimpy yellow two-piece swimming suit, looking as if she belonged on a beach in Rio instead of in staunchly conservative central Florida. She'd raise some eyebrows down at the white sand beach. Probably more than eyebrows.

After a second cup of coffee, he paid the cashier, limped outside, and stood for a few minutes in the building heat, letting the blazing sun warm his back and arms through his dark pullover shirt. He fired up a Swisher Sweet cigar. The smoke irritated the back of his throat, so he snubbed out the cigar on one of the rustic posts supporting a chain marking the limit of parking space. He flicked the dead cigar into dense green foliage at the edge of the gravel lot, then climbed into the Olds and drove for Orlando.

SOLAR TOWER was only about five stories, perhaps not tall enough to be called a tower, but it was a sleek, tinted Plexiglas and copper building that dominated the block it was on in downtown Orlando. The lobby was sparse and cool, clean except for a few cigarette butts and black heel marks on the veined marble floor. Carver studied the directory and saw that Solartown, Incorporated occupied the entire top floor. The rest of the building was leased out as office space to various smaller businesses. A doctor, a lawyer, no Indian chiefs.

Carver located the elevators only by the floor indicators on the marble wall. He'd no sooner pressed a black plastic button than a hidden door hissed softly and slid smoothly open. A tall blond woman in a black business suit smiled at him as she stepped from the elevator and hurried across the lobby toward the Orange Avenue exit. Carver watched her from the paneled and carpeted elevator until the doors slid shut. The control panel's black plastic buttons, like the one in the lobby, were numbered one through four, but the top button for the Solartown offices was marked with an illuminated yellow-orange sun that emitted rays like daggers. The button was warm beneath Carver's thumb as he depressed it and the elevator launched itself.

On the fifth floor, an elderly woman in a flowing blue dress that was supposed to make her look slimmer smiled at Carver and asked how she could help him. He explained to her only obliquely what he wanted, and she advised him that the man he should talk to was Mr. Brad Faravelli, Solartown's executive vice president in charge of development. The only hitch was, Mr. Faravelli was in a meeting.

"Everybody I want to see spends a lot of time in meetings," Carver said.

The woman, whose desk plaque declared her to be Velma Lewis, flashed him a benign smile. "Perhaps you should have phoned for an appointment."

"I should have," Carver admitted. He didn't tell her he did that as seldom as possible; in his business it was best not to afford people the opportunity to prepare for his visits.

"There's no way to know for sure when Mr. Faravelli will be free," Velma said. "But if you want to wait, I'm sure he'll see you."

Carver thanked her and limped over to a modern gray sofa that went with the building's sleek architecture. He settled into the sofa's surprising comfort and propped his cane against a glass-topped coffee table with magazines fanned out on it like an oversize poker hand. He drew an issue of *Forbes* and thumbed through it, then a slick and colorful copy of *Fortune*. For a while he read about trade imbalances, junk bonds, commodities, the relative strength of the dollar, the capitalization of Eastern Europe, and marveled at how far all that was from the world in which he moved.

By the time Velma informed him that Mr. Faravelli would see him and ushered him along an oak-paneled, carpeted hall to a spacious office, Carver felt poor.

Faravelli did nothing to assuage this. He was standing behind a massive, ornate desk and extending his hand for Carver to shake. Behind him was a wall that was all window, with narrow blinds tilted to alter the angle of the light but not to mute it. The rest of the walls were paneled like the hall, and the only decoration was a vast blowup of a color aerial photograph of

Solartown. There was very little furniture in the office. All of it was expensive.

Straining, Carver reached across the desk and shook Faravelli's strong, dry hand. Squinting into the light he was sure was designed to make him do just that and feel at a disadvantage, he studied Faravelli. What he could see of him.

The man in charge of Solartown development was about forty, average height, with thinning brown hair styled and parted on the side. His gray suit insistently whispered expensive, and there was a curious waxiness to his pale, regular features. He seemed to be only moments from suspended animation and display as an exhibit at a wax museum: American executive, circa 1990s. The sort who dressed for success down to his id.

In a pleasant voice he said, "Velma tells me you're a detective investigating a death in Solartown, Mr. Carver."

Carver confirmed that. He looked around for a place to sit down. There wasn't any. Leaning forward with both hands on the crook of his cane, feeling like a performer about to tell lewd jokes, he said, "This won't take much time. I came primarily to find out about Solartown's reverse mortgage arrangement."

Faravelli politely remained standing himself, poised and smiling. "In what context?"

Murder, Carver thought. He said, "Basically, how does the arrangement work?"

Faravelli told him in concise terms what Val Green had said earlier.

"Sounds like a profitable deal for Solartown," Carver said, probing a little with the needle.

Faravelli showed no reaction. "It can be a good deal either way. Certainly the company profits from it, but it enables us to sell homes to our retirees at prices below market value, then actually provide them with a monthly income. That we reacquire the property at the time of death doesn't matter much to the residents. And why should it?"

"What about the residents' heirs?"

Faravelli shrugged. Or his silhouette did, against the light angling through the blinds. "That's family business, not ours. To tell you the truth, Mr. Carver, we've had a few lawsuits threatened by heirs who claimed the residents were taken advantage of. All of them were dropped before reaching the courts, because there was simply no basis on which the plaintiffs could have proceeded. The fact is that our reverse mortgage plan allows retirees to turn home equity into lifelong income and maintain a desirable place to live." He extended his arms and flipped his hands palms up, as if to demonstrate there was nothing up his sleeves. "Is that such a bad thing?"

Carver limped over to where he could look at Faravelli from an angle. He could see him better without the light in his eyes. The change in their relative positions seemed to irritate Faravelli, but only mildly. Carver said, "I suppose whether it's a bad thing depends on the numbers."

Faravelli moved out from behind the desk. He had a smooth, controlled walk, like an athlete. He glanced at Carver's cane as if regretting that he was dealing with a cripple and couldn't get properly tough. Carver had seen that act before.

"I don't think I like the insinuation, Mr. Carver."

"No insinuation," Carver said, limping slowly to the side, "just an observation."

"To be blunt," Faravelli said, "I think you were implying that the reverse mortgage program is a confidence game run on the elderly."

Carver stopped his gradual sideways shuffle. The light was at his back now. Faravelli was squinting. "You seem sensitive on the subject," Carver said.

"I am!" Faravelli's voice carried more anger than he'd intended. With an effort, he modulated it. "It annoys me that every time a corporation works to help the public, the effort is misinterpreted. People like you, the media, give business a bad name, and we don't deserve it."

"Sometimes you don't," Carver admitted.

Faravelli took a deep breath, then stalked back behind his desk. He picked up an elegant pearl-gray fountain pen and jotted something on a notepad. "I'm going to do you a favor, Mr. Carver," he said as he wrote. He waved the gray memo paper a few times, then folded it in half and handed it to Carver. "Solartown is owned by five partners. This is a list of them. When you read it after leaving here, you'll see that they're hardly the type that would resort to a repugnant scam to make a few extra dollars." He screwed the cap back on the pen; Carver saw that it was gold-trimmed and monogrammed in gold. Ah, the trappings of success. Faravelli probably read and understood everything in *Forbes* and *Fortune*.

Carver tucked the folded paper into his shirt pocket and thanked Faravelli for his time. As he was limping toward the door, Faravelli said, "We sell houses to perfectly healthy couples in their fifties who might live well into their nineties. Think of that, Mr. Carver, whenever you consider a case like Maude Cranc's, where we reacquire the house after only a few years."

Carver turned around and said, "I'm surprised you're aware of individual cases."

He couldn't see Faravelli's reaction, now that he'd returned to stand behind his desk. The old back-to-the-light trick again. Upwardly mobile jerkoff must have read all the success manuals. Make your visitor feel uncomfortable, inferior, easily manipulated. The manuals didn't explain that it worked only on people who felt that way when they walked into the office. Other people it sometimes got mad. In some cases, suspicious.

Faravelli continued to stand very still, not speaking. Enough of his busy day had been consumed by this minor and unpleasant digression.

"Morning," Carver said. "It's been edifying." He limped out the door.

In the Olds he unfolded the thick gray notepaper on which Faravelli had identified the members of Solartown's partnership. They weren't names of people. In precise, slanted print, Faravelli had noted the names of an investment company, a retail clothing chain, a major bank, a lumber firm, and an insurance company. Most of them were names Carver recognized. Not at all the sort of partners that would devise what to them would be a penny-ante confidence game, not worth the effort, considering the ratio of profit to risk.

Back at the Warm Sands, Carver called Beth's room. She answered after five rings, and he wondered if she'd still been asleep. He'd known her to sleep till noon.

He read Faravelli's precise printing to her and asked her to find out what she could about Solartown and its investors.

" 'Bout time you gave me something to do," she told him. "Where you gonna be, Fred?"

He said, "Under rocks, mostly. Looking for Adam Beed."

17

CARVER PARKED the Olds on Skyview Lane, three lots up from Lou Brethwaite's rundown blue trailer. Skyview was aptly named, Carver decided, as the only view worth looking at in the trailer park just outside Orlando was the sky. Rows of single and double-wide trailers were connected by streets where grass and weeds had burst through the cracks into sunlight. Some of the trailers had decrepit wooden latticework around their bases so they resembled actual houses, but the wood had rotted away on Brethwaite's trailer and the wheels showed like guilty secrets in the shadows beneath faded blue fiberglass and rust-stained steel.

Except for a skinny young woman in a green T-shirt and baggy gray shorts, no one seemed to live on Skyview Lane. She let the screen door slam behind her on the trailer across the street from Brethwaite's, sauntered out to get her mail from a metal box that looked like a lunchbucket on top of a crooked post, then scratched her left buttock and ambled back inside. She'd only glanced at Carver, revealing she had a black eye. The homes might have wheels, but life on Skyview Lane could be an inescapable trap.

He climbed out of the Olds and limped toward Brethwaite's trailer. There were no sidewalks, and he had to be careful negotiating the slanted concrete street. After crossing the patch of weeds that passed for a front yard, he climbed three dangerous wooden steps, stood in the hot shade beneath a rusty blue and white metal awning, and knocked on the trailer door. It shook crookedly on its hinges, and the cloudy plastic that served as a window rattled noisily in its frame. Carver was afraid the opaque phony glass was going to fall out, but somehow it held. Maybe the way people here held onto life.

"Who's it?" called a voice from inside.

"Police, F.B.I., D.E.A., and Publishers Clearing House," Carver said. He knocked again, harder. The warped aluminum door shook like six kinds of Jell-O, all noisy.

A moment passed, then the door slowly opened.

Lou Brethwaite squinted out at Carver. He seemed shorter, thinner, with eyes that held nothing but pain. Carver had known him as an informer for the Orlando police. That was how Brethwaite managed to indulge his habit and stay out of prison. But the drugs were his personal prison, and he was dying there, faster now. "Fred Carver," he said, as if christening Carver. "Thought I recognized your voice, even before I peeked out the window and seen it was you."

"You don't look good, Lou," Carver said. He didn't mention that Brethwaite didn't smell good, either. The air moving from inside the trailer felt hotter than outside, and it carried the stench of sweat and urine and spicy fried food. A radio or television was on inside the trailer, tuned to a Braves game.

"I been sleeping," Brethwaite said. "You should catch me when I'm dressed to go out and I got a fresh haircut." He ran dirty fingernails through his thinning black hair. He was wearing a blue denim work shirt and incredibly wrinkled gray slacks, no shoes. A man in his twenties who could pass for forty. "Guess you're waiting for me to invite you in, huh?"

"Why don't you step out?" Carver said. "Cooler out here."

"Guess it is. Air conditioner's been busted the past month." Inside the trailer, somebody hit a double. The crowd was roaring as Brethwaite let the door slam shut.

Carver stepped down into the yard to give Brethwaite room to plod down the sagging stairs. Brethwaite stepped on a fat palmetto bug with his bare foot, but he didn't seem to notice nearly as much as the insect. Carver looked away.

"It ain't so bad seeing you now you're not a cop," Brethwaite said. "Been what, about three, four years?"

"About," Carver said. "I need some information, Lou."

Brethwaite smiled. There were more gaps in his yellowed teeth than when Carver had last seen him, not three or four years ago but last year, stoned in a bar in downtown Orlando. Still, cleaned up, after a trip to the dentist, he would have been a good-looking guy, one you'd be happy to see hanging around your sister. If you didn't know what he carried in his pockets. "I figured you didn't drop by to talk baseball, Mickey, and the Duke," he told Carver.

Carver said, "Some things never change."

Brethwaite sniffed with obvious pain, brushed at his nose with a knuckle, then examined his hand as if looking for blood. All he might see there was part of his disappearing future. Still doing coke. "That being the case, I expect you wanna pay for this information."

"A hundred in it for you, if it's good," Carver said. The sun, the smell, were beginning to get to him. He wanted to get this over with and go where it was fresh and cool. "I'm looking for a man named Adam Beed."

"No, don't do that," Brethwaite said. He frowned and spat off to the side. There was blood in his spittle. Some of it dribbled down onto his chin. "He's a fella best not found."

"Nevertheless," Carver said.

"Yeah. Well, I won't pretend I ain't scared to tell you, but it don't matter how I feel, 'cause I don't know where you might latch onto Beed."

Carver drew two fifty-dollar bills from his pocket and held them creased over his forefinger.

Brethwaite glanced at the bills and gave his yellow smile. "Keep your hundred, stay alive, I'll stay alive, that's the best way this conversation can go. Beed's a genuine through-an'-through bad-ass, Carver. Last I heard he was outa prison and on booze so as to stay legal and not violate parole."

"He's broken parole. Otherwise I'd be able to find him."

"Well, running out on your parole officer's not the best play, but that's not the same as chancing going back behind the walls on a drug charge. Beed got clean enough in prison that he's an alky now." Again the ruined smile. "It's a more socially acceptable substance, not to mention legal, but despite the fact he's a physical fitness freak, he's just as addicted as ever and eventually it'll take him down. An addict's an addict, legal drug or not. I don't shit myself or anybody else about that. Thing is, Beed don't run in any of his old circles these days. That's why I can't tell you where you might find him, or even who else might know."

Carver slipped the hundred into his pocket, watching Brethwaite stare at it until it disappeared. He was wasted and dying and needed the money; he was telling the truth.

"You ever consider going into a rehab program, Lou?" Carver asked. Had Oprah Winfrey ever considered a diet?

"I'm on a waiting list. Been on it for eight months." Staring down at his dirty bare feet, Brethwaite sniffled again and said, "I do have something for you might be worth one of them fifties."

Carver pulled out one of the bills and held it between thumb and forefinger. He knew Brethwaite, knew he was about to part with fifty dollars' worth of truth. In a perverted way, his honesty kept him alive day to day, the currency he exchanged for dollars.

"I heard a guy crossed Beed a few months back down in Miami—don't ask me how or why, 'cause I don't know. I only tell you what I *do* know. Anyway, you ever see that movie where the dude who crossed the Mafia wakes up one fine morning and finds a horse's head next to him in bed?"

Carver nodded.

"Well, this guy in Miami found his wife's head resting on her pillow like usual, but nothing else under the covers. Still ain't found the rest of her," Brethwaite's lips danced as he stared hard at Carver. "That give you an idea what kinda geek you're looking for?"

Carver handed him the fifty, then turned around and limped back to the car. His stomach didn't feel so good, and he hated the fear that hindered his limbs like arthritis.

"Helluva movie, anyway," Brethwaite said behind him, an instant before the trailer's flimsy door slammed shut and rattled.

Carver was in more of a mood for a musical.

18

AFTER LEAVING Lou Brethwaite, Carver phoned Lloyd Van Meter from a booth on Silver Star Road. Van Meter was one of the more successful private investigators in Florida, with offices in Miami, Tampa, and Orlando. He agreed to meet Carver that evening at Bixby's Lounge on Magnolia Avenue.

The night was hot and thick as gauze when Carver parked in Bixby's lot, then limped into the lounge through the wide entrance flanked by flickering neon palm trees.

It was almost cold in Bixby's; it felt like ice being applied where Carver's shirt was plastered to his flesh with perspiration. The spacious main room was starting to fill with the late-night crowd. Most of the round tables were occupied, the five-piece band had started playing, and half a dozen couples were dancing slowly on the small square floor in back. It wouldn't be long before the music and the dancing would accelerate in noise and motion. Right now, Carver thought, Bixby's seemed comparatively peaceful. Stillness before storm.

It was easy to spot Van Meter's 300-plus pounds perched on a stool near the end of the long mahogany and glass-brick bar. He was wearing a green suit with a muted gray chalk stripe, green leather loafers with silver-tipped toes, a yellow shirt with what looked in the back bar mirror to be a red and green tie. He noticed Carver in the mirror and turned and smiled. He had a broad face and flowing white beard that with his bulk lent him an authoritative, biblical air, like one of those color illustrations in a dime-store religious tract. His commanding presence, his vivid awning-size clothes, as usual took Carver aback for a moment. There sat Moses sipping a beer after a spree through the K-mart men's department.

They shook hands and Carver took the stool next to him, hooking the crook of his cane over the bar's leather elbow rest. The bartender came and took his order for a Budweiser.

"You seem agitated," Van Meter said. "Your same feisty self only more so."

"I've got a problem," Carver said.

"Guys like you have always got those."

"His name's Adam Beed."

Van Meter stroked his beard, sipped his beer. "That's a problem, all right."

"You've heard of him?"

"Sure. In a darkly legendary way. Like Vlad the Impaler. Never met the legend and I got no desire to." He grinned at Carver. "But I guess I'm gonna, right?"

"Not exactly," Carver said. "I only need you to locate him." The bartender brought his Bud, poured exactly half of it into a glass as carefully as if it were an explosive, and walked away. Carver lifted the glass, said "Cheers," and downed most of the beer.

"Why would you want to find Adam Beed?" Van Meter asked.

"Because he found me," Carver said.

Van Meter stared at him but didn't push it.

"Has to do with a job I'm on out in Solartown," Carver said. He gave Van Meter a brief summary of the case.

"The old folks at play," Van Meter said. Then he glanced at his hulking gray reflection in the mirror and sighed. "Well, I'm getting there myself. Just like you, Fred. Like us all."

Carver didn't want to wax melancholy over advancing age. He said, "My drug contacts aren't going to do me any good. Beed's a physical health nut, a weight lifter and martial arts expert in a major way. He's also off illegal narcotics, making his drug of choice alcohol these days. Fanatically disciplined as he is, and worshiping his own muscles, he must have a helluva battle with booze. Control freaks always do. And there seems no doubt he's an alcoholic."

"A killing machine that drinks," Van Meter reflected. "Now there's a dangerous combination."

"I'm not asking you to take away his car keys," Carver said. "I got pressures that keep me from spending time tracking him down. You've got more contacts, people working for you. You can check with AA chapters, gyms, martial arts studios, much easier than I can."

"It'll take time," Van Meter said. "This one'll have to cost you, Fred. Gotta cover my expenses."

"I didn't expect it for free," Carver told him.

"You mentioned Beth was working with you on this."

Carver nodded.

"I'll help you on it, just so she don't get mixed up in looking for Beed. I heard about something he's supposed to have done a few months ago down in Miami."

"Me, too."

"Scary, huh?"

Carver shrugged. "People like Beed are part of the work we do."

"The work *I* do, in this instance."

"You afraid to take the job?" Carver asked.

Van Meter leaned back on his stool, looking astonished and slightly angry, as if he might pull the Ten Commandments out of a pocket and set Carver straight on a few things. "Fred, Fred, you insult me. I'll assign someone else to it."

Carver smiled. "You're getting smarter as the years pass."

"Not you, Fred. That's how come I worry about you. Why I worry about Beth, who seems to suffer from some of the same rash impulses. We need to concern ourselves with Beth, since Adam Beed's involved in what you're mucking around in. From what I've heard, he's a kinky kinda homicidal maniac who's got no love for women. His mother must have drop-kicked him or something. The shrinks might say he looks at a woman, even a woman like Beth, and sees his mother. Sets him off, maybe."

"I'm not interested in his tortured childhood," Carver said, "even if he had one and it had anything to do with what he did to that guy's wife down in Miami."

"Guess it ain't really relevant now," Van Meter admitted. He picked up Carver's Budweiser bottle and poured beer into the glass in Carver's hand. "Here, pal, let me put a head on that for you."

BETH WAS in his bed when he got back to the motel. Carver wasn't sure how he felt about that. He remembered what Van Meter had said about rash impulses.

"You don't seem surprised to see me," she said.

He shut the door and limped farther into the room. "Not much surprises me anymore, even on my birthday. How'd you get in?"

"Locks don't concern me much, Fred."

He leaned on his cane and looked at her in the light of the bedside reading lamp. The air conditioner was humming away on high, and she was lying on her back and covered almost to the neck with the sheet. Her lithe body seemed incredibly long.

Her shoulders were bare and he was sure she was nude beneath the white cotton. She'd been reading before he'd arrived; a thick paperback book was propped open on the table that held the lamp. Something by Joseph Conrad.

After his conversation with Van Meter, it bothered him that she'd chanced being seen so they could be together for the night. Besides that, he'd stayed too long at Bixby's, drunk several more beers and talked too much with Van Meter. He was feeling less than amorous. "It was a risk, you coming here."

"Everything's a risk, from birth to death, even if you're a suburban WASP and you've got your life arranged so you don't know it."

"You sure nobody saw you?"

"Positive. I float like a shadow through the heart of darkness."

"Some shadow."

"It's almost eleven o'clock, Fred, and I smell beer on you all the way over here. Where you been?"

"Drinking with Lloyd Van Meter."

"Ah! You hiring him to help locate Adam Beed?"

"Uh-huh. You have any luck finding out about Solartown, Inc.'s major shareholders?"

"I don't rely on luck, Fred." She ran a long-nailed finger slowly across her lower lip. "C'mon to bed, lover. Business later."

He wondered, what could there be about Joseph Conrad? Then he got undressed and joined her, becoming unexpectedly aroused when he felt the heat of her beneath the thin sheet. His knuckles brushed the smooth, warm expanse of her thigh.

Her hand found him and did its magic. "Knew you'd see it my way," she said, and slid on top of him.

It was morning before he thought again about Jerome Evans or his widow Hattie or Adam Beed or Joseph Conrad. Or anything other than Beth.

She was good at that.

19

WHILE BETH was showering the next morning, Carver drove down the highway to a doughnut shop and bought half a dozen glazed and a large cup of coffee to go.

When he returned, she was wearing panties and bra and drying her hair with a big white towel from the still-steamy bathroom. She sniffed the air and eyed the doughnut bag. "Smells yummy."

He put the grease-spotted bag and the cup on the desk.

"Only one cup?" she said.

"Only one occupant in this room," he reminded her. He limped into the bathroom, ripped the plastic sanitary wrap from one of the glasses, and carried the glass back out to the desk. He poured about half of the large cup of coffee into it, leaving it black. "I brought you some powdered cream," he said, "only the label calls it 'Mock Milk.' "

"Sounds heavenly, if only you remembered a plastic spoon."

He found himself wondering if she was recalling her luxurious existence with Roberto Gomez, when coffee was no doubt brought to her and the spoons were silver, from the largest serving size down to the tiniest coke spoons worn on delicate neck chains.

When she was finished with her hair, she slipped into a pair of shorts and a clean orange blouse, then dragged over a chair to sit across from him at the desk. She sprinkled cream in her coffee, stirred it gingerly with her finger, and they went to work on breakfast.

"Fresh," she commented, through a mouthful of glazed doughnut.

"I'm working on that," he said.

"If I wanted bad comedy," she told him, "I'd tune in to local news."

After finishing his second doughnut, he wiped sugar glaze from his hands with a napkin and settled back with his coffee. He said, "Tell me about Solartown."

She swallowed a last bite of doughnut, then licked a long finger. "The five principal shareholders are all players in the financial major leagues. We're talking a prestigious investment company, a bank with international holdings, a lumber firm that's one of the largest in the world, a retail chain with stores in half the states, and an insurance company that has more money than most small countries. All of them, with the possible exception of the bank, are on solid financial footing. Solartown's a minor part of their overall picture."

"How'd you learn all this?"

"It's mostly public information, available at the touch of a few computer keys."

"Your friend Jeff's computer?"

"His and mine. The laptop I use to compose when I travel has a modem. I also called some contacts I have in various high positions. People I knew from when I was with Roberto."

"Users?"

She nodded. "But dependable."

"Not to their employers."

"None of them runs a train, Fred. Don't be so damned judgmental."

"I wasn't passing judgment, only wondering how good your information is."

"It's good as it gets. And what it means is that, unless there's some small fish with ideas of his or her own, Solartown, Inc. is too friggin' big to be operating some scam to do old folks outa their houses so they can resell them. That'd be like you and me hanging around schoolyards to swipe lunch money."

"Lunch money's stolen every day," Carver said. "What about Brad Faravelli? He's in a perfect position to steal from the other kids."

"He seems okay, but who knows? Forty-two years old, married, three kids, Harvard Business School grad, been with Solartown since it began seven years ago. Before that he was a vice prez at a Wall Street investment company that went belly-up over some questionable bond trading. He wasn't directly involved in it, by the way."

Carver said, "Harvard. Wall Street. Jesus!"

"Don't be a reverse snob, Fred. Anyway, I can get a better feel for it all after I interview Faravelli this afternoon. I told him I'm doing a feature story for *Burrow*, but it might be published in some other Florida papers, as well."

"He believed that?" Carver asked.

"It might be the truth, Fred." She finished her coffee, then wadded her napkin and stuffed it into the empty foam cup. There was a crescent of red from her lipstick on the cup's rim. "What about you?" she asked. "You were your usual unbleeding, unconcussed self last night, and you'd talked with Van Meter about him locating Adam Beed. So I'm assuming you didn't run into Beed yourself, or find out much about him."

He realized for the first time she'd risked coming to his room because she was concerned about him. Not one of her rash impulses at all.

"Beed seems to have really gotten off drugs while he was in Raiford," he said. "He's strictly a boozer now."

"Same thing, different terminology. He's an addict, if the booze is running him. He's as outa control as if he were on coke or heroin."

"It doesn't seem to have that kind of hold on him."

"Not yet. But if he's drinking regularly, it'll get him."

"That a prediction?"

"I've seen it plenty of times. A junkie shakes the physical dependency and fancies he's no longer part of the world of drugs, but it's okay to have drinks with dinner, or duck into a bar now and then for a couple of something cool. All socially acceptable. Then the alcohol takes the place of whatever else he was on, takes him over body and mind just like any other drug." She tapped a red fingernail on the desk for emphasis. "An addict's an addict, Fred. Like a cucumber that's become a pickle. It can never be a cucumber again. Even longtime users sometimes kid themselves they're cucumbers again, but if they don't stay away from drugs altogether, including alcohol, it'll eventually kill them."

The air conditioner had gone through a short cycle, then kicked off. Carver, sitting in the sudden silence, hadn't realized it was running. A child began yammering outside, then car doors slammed and an engine started. Tires crunched over gravel as a vacationing family got an early start.

"Eventually, but *always*," Beth said.

Carver said, "It's nice to know that about Beed."

AFTER BREAKFAST he left Beth preparing for her interview with Brad Faravelli and drove over to see Hattie Evans.

As he was parking, he saw her in the shade of her front porch. She was wearing baggy jeans and an oversize T-shirt with GRAY POWER lettered on it, tending to flowers in a plastic hanging planter she'd taken down from its hook.

"Care to come inside, Mr. Carver?" she asked, not looking at him until he'd limped almost to her.

"Don't let me interrupt you," he said. "We might as well enjoy it out here before the sun and the temperature get higher."

"That won't take long," she said, pinching off a dead geranium. "Gotta water these constantly. Florida. It was Jerome's idea to move down here, not mine."

"You intend to stay?"

"Not much choice, considering the mortgage arrangement we made with Solartown."

"Whose idea was that?"

"Jerome's. He handled all our finances. In retrospect, it was dumb of me to let him do that."

"You're a capable woman," Carver said. "You can set things right."

"Not this house. But then, I suppose I'm happy enough here in Solartown."

"When you bought the house, did the salesman give you the hard sell on the reverse mortgage?"

"Not really. There was no deception involved."

"Did Jerome ever look into another form of financing? I mean, do you know if he consulted with a lender in the months before his death?"

She picked up a gray metal watering can with a daisy design on it. "Not that I know of." She tipped the can so the long, thin spout was out of sight among the remaining flowers, letting water flow into the pot. "That's not to say Jerome might not have seen a banker without telling me." She shot Carver a look he couldn't interpret. "Seems he did other things without informing me."

Carver said nothing.

Water flowed over the rim of the pot and along the porch rail.

"I might have to leave town for a while," he told her, "if someone I have working for me locates a man who could be important to us."

"That Adam Beed?"

He nodded.

Hattie set the watering can down and removed her green vinyl work gloves. The gloves had oversize cuffs with the same daisy design that was on the can. "The people involved in this made a mistake trying to scare you off the case, didn't they?"

"Looks that way," he said.

"Can't say I'm shocked that you're still on the job. You reminded me immediately of some of my problem students who regarded intimidation as merely a temporary condition. Much as I regretted their presence in my classes, after all the years they're the ones I remember."

"Memory's a strange thing," Carver said.

"A precious thing," she said, surprising him.

"Your emotions are showing, Hattie."

She gave him a sad smile, standing there erect and holding her gloves folded in one hand as if she were a military officer. She said, "I missed out on some things in life, Mr. Carver; I've come to accept that because I understand it. Now I need to know about my husband's death, so I can accept it through understanding and fit it peacefully in my past. So I won't wake up before sunrise every morning thinking about it for the rest of my life."

"I see what you mean," Carver said.

"I believe you do." She lifted the watering can again and gently doused the blossoms themselves.

"Where's your neighbor Val Green today?"

She glared at him. "How should I know? Why should I care about the old busybody?"

He almost smiled. "Better not talk that way; you might wilt those flowers."

"He tells me if I need anything to call him or come get him, as if I need the likes of him to take care of me. As if I need anyone."

"You're not being fair to him. He's not a bad sort."

"Oh, I suppose he's all right," she said. "In his place. I expect he's sleeping. I think he was driving around last night playing policeman."

"You don't think much of the Posse?"

"I think they're a bunch of old fools who've regressed to childhood, playing cops and robbers again. Now Val, he even wants to play doctor."

Carver laughed. Some of the water sloshed out of the long-spouted can and splashed near his shoe. Not an accident, he was sure.

"Well, it happens to be true." Hattie put down the can and concentrated hard on rehanging the planter on its eye hook. Either her eyesight wasn't up to it, or the hook was moving.

Carver thought about offering to help, then decided she might resent it. He waited until the planter was dangling safely on its chain.

"If I have to disappear for a while, I'll call you," he assured her.

"You'd better. I hired you."

She stretched to take down an identical plastic planter from the opposite side of the porch, and he said good-bye and left her there.

As he drove away he glanced over at her. She wasn't watching him. She was plucking dead blossoms.

20

ON THE drive back to the motel, Carver detoured past Maude Crane's house. There was a red and white Solartown Realty FOR SALE sign reflecting sun in the neatly mowed front yard. He wasn't sure if that meant Maude had bought on the reverse mortgage plan and ownership of her house had reverted to the company. It was something worth looking into.

At the Warm Sands, Carver found that Beth had already left for her interview with Brad Faravelli, and there were no messages either from her or Van Meter.

The room felt cool and he realized he was sweating. He limped into the bathroom and splashed cold water on his face. When he glanced at himself in the mirror he saw that his normally deep tan was even deeper from running around Solartown and environs asking questions. The possibility of future skin cancer leapt to mind, all those TV talk shows and infomercials, and he felt himself moving closer to seriously considering Hattie's advice about headwear to cover his bald pate. But then, he had Adam Beed to deal with before measuring a future in years instead of days.

He put on a fresh shirt and decided to go see Desoto, offer to buy him lunch and then pump him to find out if he knew anything else about Beed or Solartown. What friends were for.

But Desoto, perched on the edge of his desk and just hanging up his phone, said he was busy. There'd been a homicide out near the Orlando Country Club; he'd just returned from there.

"A shooting that left a hole in one?" Carver asked.

Desoto gave him a fierce and pitying look that let him know this was no time for cop humor, not even the kind that saves sanity. Carver felt microscopically small when Desoto explained what had happened.

A teenage girl had been raped and strangled, not necessarily in that order. Desoto was charging around barking orders, his dark eyes sad and furious. It upset him when any crime of violence was committed against a woman. Something like this, involving a young girl, really set him off. He wouldn't have time for Carver today. Carver didn't blame him. Desoto had seen the body.

The day was heating up to near-record temperatures, and Carver hated himself for his insensitivity and was feeling frustrated. He loathed spinning his wheels, and so far today he'd found no traction. He left the Olds parked on Hughey near police headquarters and walked up to South Street to eat lunch at a restaurant he remembered.

Halfway there he realized he was limping along faster than most people were walking, drawing stares and working up a sweat that ran in rivulets. Breathing hard, too. Punishing himself. He made himself slow down, determined not to let the futility of the day get to him. It had been one of the hardest things in life for him to learn, not to be his own enemy. Sometimes he still forgot the lesson.

He had chili for lunch, another wrong decision. When he left the restaurant, he found a public phone at the corner and stood miserably in the exhaust fumes and terrible sun. He called the Warm Sands Motel and asked for Beth's extension.

Ah! She'd returned from her Faravelli interview.

"Faravelli spent most of our time together bragging about Solartown," she said. "A real PR guy. He made the most of the interview."

"You get into the reverse mortgage arrangement?" Carver asked.

"Far as I could, without him suspecting I was targeting it. He gave me some straight information. Made a good case that the purpose of the program was not only to sell more houses, but to improve the quality of life for buyers by providing them with a better home than they might otherwise be able to afford, plus a monthly income for the rest of their natural lives."

"Sounds good when you say it fast."

"That's how he said it. He's a charmer when he wants to turn it on."

"Doesn't it figure?"

"Maybe not. You want my opinion, Fred, the guy seems like a legitimate corporate climber. He might doctor reports or evict old ladies to improve the bottom line, but I don't see him getting involved in murder unless there's some kinda blackmail being worked."

"Always a possibility with such an upright citizen."

"Such a cynic."

"I get called that a lot. People are thoughtless that way."

"Where are you, Fred? You finally buy yourself a car phone?"

"I'm in Orlando talking at one of those outside phones. That's why you hear traffic. You get any figures on the percentage of houses Solartown repossesses after the owner's death?"

"Easy," she said. "A hundred percent."

"Huh?"

"About half the homes in Solartown are sold on the reverse mortgage plan. The loans are amortized at a thirty-year rate. Virtually no retiree who buys will live the full thirty years. How much profit or loss Solartown makes on the repossessed houses depends on how long the occupants collect the monthly payments and how much the houses appreciate. In effect, Solartown's buying back the house from the owner, until the owner's death, which will always occur before the full price is paid."

"You don't see that as a motive?"

"I would, Fred, if I could make the numbers add up to the point where the profit was worth the risk of being found out and ruining a much more lucrative legitimate enterprise. It simply looks like a winning situation for both parties, a marketing angle Faravelli boasts about with some justification."

Carver wondered if Faravelli had been even charming enough to fool Beth. That seemed impossible. But so did the collapse of the Soviet Union, and here we were. He said, "I noticed Maude Crane's house is for sale."

"Matter of fact, Faravelli mentioned that one. It's been taken back by the company, and he admits they'll realize a large profit on it. Said it was an example of what made it possible for Solartown to lower its profit margin on newer housing and undersell competitors. Good fortune growing from misfortune, he called it."

"I'm wondering if it's somebody's personal fortune," Carver said.

"Uh-huh. You want me to follow the money, Fred?"

"Can you do it?"

"Won't be easy. Banks are secretive."

"But money can always be traced, and I know you have your wily ways."

"I have those," she admitted, "but I can't promise you they'll work. Banks weren't computerized, this might not be possible."

"I'm not asking you to do anything illegal."

She laughed. "Don't try to bullshit me, Fred."

"Okay, I'm asking you not to get caught."

"That's my Fred." She hung up.

Carver called the Warm Sands again, this time identifying himself, and asked if there were any messages for him.

There was one: He was supposed to call a Mr. Van Meter as soon as possible.

Ah, traction! That would mean direction. The day's prospects were improving.

Not minding the heat and exhaust fumes now, or the persistent aftertaste of the chili, he fished in his pocket for change.

VAN METER said a contact in a detox center in Jacksonville reported that a woman with delirium tremens had muttered Adam Beed's name. Beed had done something to her, but she wouldn't say what, and when she'd regained her composure she wouldn't talk about him at all. She was scared sober, the detox guy had said. But while drunk she'd mentioned being with Beed near the ocean in a tall pink building in Lauderdale-by-the-Sea, and she kept holding up her right hand with two missing fingers and saying something that sounded like "Hen power."

"You sober yourself?" Carver asked, watching a pickup truck towing a trailer thread dangerously through traffic at high speed. Idiot! Where was a cop when you needed one? Out by the golf course.

"There's a tall pink building on Ocean Boulevard in Lauderdale called the Heron Tower," Van Meter said.

"It's flamingos that are pink."

"Sure, but try to make 'hen power' out of 'flamingo.' "

"Is Beed listed at that address?"

"No, but he wouldn't be using his real name. I don't know

if it all means anything, Fred. Up to you if you wanna drive over and check."

"What's your gut tell you?" Carver asked.

"Besides that I'm hungry?"

"Besides."

"Hen power," Van Meter said.

He gave Carver the address.

21

CARVER RENTED a Plymouth from Budget Rent-a-Car in Fort Lauderdale and drove to nearby Lauderdale-by-the-Sea.

There was the Heron Tower at the address Van Meter had given him, a sleek building about twenty stories high that was constructed mainly of cast concrete embedded with what looked like pink seashells. The front of the building faced North Ocean Boulevard, the back looked out on the Atlantic. Pink-tinted glass doors flanked by columns resembling busty mermaids formed the entrance. Off to the side was a narrow concrete driveway that led to ground-level parking beneath the building, a shadowy cavern with concrete pillars that acted as piers supporting the entire structure.

After sitting in the parked blue Plymouth for fifteen minutes, Carver decided there was no doorman. He waited another fifteen minutes, until dusk had become darkness, then he climbed out of the Plymouth, hobbled quickly across North Ocean Boulevard to beat the traffic, and entered Heron Tower.

The lobby was mostly a checkered pattern of gray and black

marble veined in pale pink. It was swank, but it reminded Carver of a marble chess set he'd bought years ago in Mexico. The pawns cracked easily.

He limped across the bare floor to the bank of mailboxes and intercoms, his footsteps and the tapping of his cane echoing over hard surfaces.

It was difficult to guess which of the names in the slots above the mailboxes might be Adam Beed's alias. Most of the slots contained the names of women or families. An even half-dozen contained only men's names. Alan Brake, in the penthouse, seemed a likely possibility. Same initials. Beed was getting plenty of money from somewhere and living high, so why not the penthouse?

An elderly couple walking a practically bald poodle entered the lobby and glanced at Carver as they waited for the elevator. When they'd gone upstairs, he made a note of the six male names, then returned to the Plymouth and sat with the motor idling and the air conditioner humming away on high. He wouldn't draw much attention where he was parked, so he settled back and let himself slide into his waiting mode, a sort of state of relaxation combined with an acute awareness of what was going on around him. It was a systematic shutting down of those parts of the mind not needed for the task and was a knack you developed after dozens of stakeouts; he thought sometimes it might be a form of self-hypnosis. Whatever it was, every good cop had it, and it allowed him to tolerate hours of stillness and waiting with the self-contained patience of a sniper.

Tenants and visitors came and went at the Heron Tower, none of them without Carver noticing.

When the sun had been down for about an hour, the evening finally began to cool and he switched off the engine and air conditioner and cranked down the Plymouth's front windows. A gentle, fetid breeze that smelled of the ocean worked its way through the car. He turned on the radio and played the push buttons, momentarily hearing a Spanish station and thinking of Desoto.

He switched the radio off as he saw a new black Cadillac Seville slow down and then turn into the Heron Tower driveway. Carver watched the car's bright taillights disappear into the bowels of the building, like wary red eyes sinking below ground level. He was sure Adam Beed had been behind the wheel.

Quickly Carver climbed out of the Plymouth, hobbled across the street, and entered the Heron Tower lobby. Planting the tip of his cane carefully on the smooth marble floor, he stood off to the side and watched the digital floor indicators above the two elevators.

One of the elevators descended from the third floor to garage level, then began to rise.

Carver had an uneasy moment as it reached the lobby. There was nowhere to conceal himself if Beed had decided to take a walk or go out and buy a bottle before going up to his apartment, and got out of the elevator.

But the elevator rose past the lobby. Carver watched it stop at the fifteenth floor. The number fifteen continued to glow in orange letters above the elevator.

After a few minutes Carver limped from the lobby and returned to the Plymouth. He checked his list of male tenants. There was only one living on the fifteenth floor: Bernard Altman. Okay, Adam Beed's initials reversed. The apartment number was 15-B. Carver had calculated the Heron Tower numbering system and figured it had to be a corner unit overlooking the beach and ocean.

He drove around the block and parked farther up the street, where he could see an illuminated window on the fifteenth floor. The window faced north and was just around the corner from a small balcony that provided a view of the sea. No movement behind the window was visible, but the light itself suggested there was someone home and it was the right apartment. Beed wasn't likely to raise the blinds and pose for Carver.

Well, maybe, if he knew someone was watching.

After about twenty minutes a figure did pass the window. Even in silhouette, Carver recognized the bulk and confident carriage of Adam Beed.

Carver kept an eye on the apartment until almost ten o'clock, getting out and walking around every now and then, once buying a cup of frozen yogurt from a shop down the block and sitting on a bench with it for a while, so he wouldn't appear suspicious if anyone did notice him. The street here was mostly condos and apartment buildings, some with shops on the lower floors, but more tourists than tenants were driving past or wandering the sidewalks. All of them seemed too preoccupied to pay much attention to Carver.

Finally he decided Beed was in for the night, so he drove up 1A1 to the Sandy Shoes Motel on El Mar Drive, where he'd registered earlier.

After stripping down to his underwear, he arranged for a wake-up call at six the next morning, then stretched out on his back, lay listening to the breaking surf, and fell asleep.

HE HAD to sit in the parked Plymouth for more than an hour the next morning before seeing Adam Beed drive from the Heron Tower parking garage in his black Cadillac.

Carver started the Plymouth's engine and pulled out into traffic behind the Caddy, driving with the window open in the still-cool morning. It was going to be a beautiful day even if oven temperature; sunlight glinted off chrome and glass and concrete and made everything seem new and clean. The brightly and casually clad vacationers and locals strolling along the sidewalk were chatting and smiling. Joggers bounced with vivaciousness, birds sang, a soft breeze blew, gulls screamed with unbridled joy. It was a fine morning to be following a monster.

He stayed well back, switching lanes from time to time, making sure Beed wouldn't notice the unobtrusive blue car in his rearview mirror. Plymouths like this were rented by the hundreds in central Florida; that was why Carver had requested one.

Beed steered the Cadillac into the parking lot of the Big 'n' Yum restaurant on Talmont Avenue. Carver drove past, parked down the block, and walked back.

He stood across the street and studied the Big 'n' Yum. It appeared to be a topless bar at night and a restaurant that served breakfast and lunch during the day. A sign proclaimed the daylight specials to be topless egg-and-sausage sandwiches until 10:00 A.M., then hamburgers on topless buns until 5:00. It was the kind of entrepreneurship Carver admired.

The Big 'n' Yum was indeed large, a low brick building with planters along the sills of windows that had been walled up to leave rectangles of newer, lighter bricks. Long vines dangled from the planters, but Carver saw no flowers. There were six such windows and planters on the long side of the rectangular building, bordering the parking lot where Adam Beed's Cadillac sat among half a dozen other cars and a yellow Isuzu off-road vehicle, all gleaming in the sun as if they were freshly painted.

With so few customers apparently inside, Carver didn't think he should risk entering the restaurant. He also didn't want to push things by sitting nearby in the parked car. Unremarkable as the rental car was, Adam Beed might remember glimpsing it near the Heron Tower, or driving behind him this morning.

He bought a *Sun Sentinel* from a vending machine and sat down on a small stone wall that ran in front of a travel agency that seemed to be closed. A kid about twelve wandered by wearing a Tampa Marlins baseball cap. Carver spun him a tale about being a fan and bought the cap for ten dollars. The kid was astounded and happy. He'd rush home and tell his mom or dad; they'd never figure it out.

Carver sat wearing the billed cap, head bowed, pretending to study the newspaper in his lap. The bill, the covered baldness, made for good camouflage. Even if Beed looked hard, he wouldn't be able to identify him from this distance.

About nine o'clock, when Carver's pelvis was beginning to go numb from contact with the low stone wall, Beed and a barrel-chested, dark-haired man in an expensive blue suit emerged from the restaurant. The man was short, and he looked squat and diminutive alongside Beed's muscular bulk, like a noontime shadow. They stood on the sunny sidewalk and talked for a few minutes, each listening intently to the other. Then they shook hands and Beed got into the Caddy. He started the motor but didn't drive away until the well-dressed, stocky man climbed into the Isuzu and drove from the lot.

For a moment Carver wondered if he should follow the Isuzu, but he decided to stay with Adam Beed. That was why he'd come here, right? He put the yellow Isuzu out of his mind.

Beed drove to a drugstore on Sunrise and bought a newspaper and a small item Carver couldn't make out from where he stood near the magazine rack.

Carver limped back to the Plymouth before Beed came back out into the sun and climbed into the Caddy. Beed had walked from the drugstore with a sense of purpose, and he drove that way, too. The Cadillac kept to the speed limit, wove through traffic to Langdon Street, in a wealthy suburb east of town, and parked in front of a large stucco house with a green tile roof and green canvas awnings. Number seventeen, according to black iron scrollwork near the driveway.

Carver found an unobtrusive spot to park in the shade and watched Beed get out of the Caddy and stride toward the house with all the confidence and determination of a man selling encyclopedias.

He stayed inside until almost noon, and when he came back out he had his dark suit coat slung over his bulky shoulder and was carrying a tan leather briefcase. He tossed the briefcase on the passenger-side front seat of the Cadillac, then walked around and got in behind the steering wheel.

Carver followed him to a restaurant near the ocean and sat sweltering in the parking lot while Beed ate lunch. Then he kept him in sight while Beed drove back to the Heron Tower and jockeyed the Caddy into the concealing shadows of the parking garage.

After fifteen minutes, Carver figured Beed would stay home for a while and drove to a McDonald's. He ordered a low-calorie McLean burger, large fries, and a chocolate milkshake, figuring it was a good day for irony if not cholesterol, and what the hell, he hadn't had breakfast.

When he returned to the Heron Tower, he drove into the garage to make sure Beed's Cadillac was still there. He didn't want to park back out on the street and sit in the car until Beed left again, and he was sure to draw attention if he parked there in the garage.

He sat in the coolness of the garage with the Plymouth's motor idling, thinking it all over, then he drove back out into the brilliant sunlight and down the street to a strip of souvenir shops. He bought a couple of large beach towels, swimming trunks, a cap, and a T-shirt. The cap had LIFE'S A BEACH lettered on it. The T-shirt proclaimed GOOD HAPPENS.

AFTER PAYING for everything, he put the trunks on beneath his pants in the changing room, explaining to the clerk that he wanted to go directly to the public beach. Then he drove back to the Heron Tower and parked down the street. He slipped out of his pants, shirt, and socks in the car, banging his elbow on the steering wheel and dash. Then he put his moccasins back on and got out of the car. He stuck the cap on his head, thinking of Hattie.

Carrying the wadded towels and T-shirt, he cut through the lobby of the hotel two buildings down from the Heron Tower and limped the short distance to the beach. For all anyone knew, he was a guest; and he was wearing the kind of attitude that didn't invite inquiry.

The beach was crowded with sunbathers, kids building odd structures in the sand, young lovers letting people know it, and several teenagers tossing Frisbees that threatened to spin out of control and decapitate entire families. Keeping to the wet and firmly packed sand just beyond the surf line, Carver limped parallel to the sea and found a spot on the beach near the back of the Heron Tower, where he could see the driveway from the parking garage.

He spread out one of the towels and weighted it down with his moccasins. Then he peeled his T-shirt over his head, stuffed it in his cap so the wind wouldn't take it, and laid it on the spread-out towel next to the other, wadded towel.

In the interest of realism he limped to the water's edge and left his cane jutting from the sand. He went for a short swim, not very far out, then came back and stretched out on his stomach on the towel, wishing he'd bought some sunscreen and keeping an eye on the black Caddy he could barely make out in the angle between the Heron Tower garage's concrete pillars.

After a while he spread the other towel over him to protect against sunburn, plunked the cap tightly over his bald head, and settled down like a hunter in a blind, which in fact he was.

IT WAS almost five o'clock when he saw Adam Beed walking through the garage toward the Cadillac.

Carver shoved his bare feet into his moccasins and used his cane to stand up as he grabbed towels and T-shirt. He hobbled as fast as he could back into the hotel lobby and through to the street to where the Plymouth was parked. He was trailing sand and drawing some stares now, but it didn't matter.

As he reached the car, he saw that Beed had already pulled from the garage and the Caddy was turning the corner at the end of the block. Carver got the Plymouth going and cut over a cross street at close to fifty miles an hour.

As he made a right turn he saw the black Caddy in front of him, about a block away.

He relaxed and followed.

BEED MET the same short, stocky man he'd seen at breakfast. They had dinner at a small Cuban restaurant downtown. Like the topless lounge this morning, this was the kind of place a man dressed as well as Beed's companion—and for that matter Beed—didn't figure to frequent. And there seemed to be something furtive in their mannerisms. Carver considered that they might be homosexual lovers meeting on the sly, but despite Beed's background in prison, that didn't quite ring true. There was nothing in the glances they exchanged, and there was no touching. The relationship seemed more businesslike than personal. Still, it would be interesting to see if they went their separate ways when they left the restaurant.

They did. But not before Beed had removed the leather briefcase from the trunk of the Caddy and placed it in the back of the yellow Isuzu.

The barrel-chested man in the business suit sat for a few minutes in the Isuzu, then drove away last, as soon as Beed's black Cadillac had disappeared.

This time Carver followed the yellow Isuzu.

22

THE SQUARISH little yellow vehicle was easy to keep in sight as it cut east, then made its way north on 1A1 along the shoreline. Carver noticed for the first time that there was a small dog in the Isuzu. Occasionally it would leap up to lick the driver's face. It was too far away for Carver to see what breed it might be, but it appeared to have short hair. Once the man, still staring straight ahead at the road, reached over and ruffled the dog behind the ears. The dog shimmied its neck and head as if trying to shake off the sensation.

Carver drove with the windows down, now and then glancing to his right at the ocean rolling its inexhaustible life out on the beach. From here the splaying white surf appeared pure, unsullied by the debris carried in on the swells, the blackened seaweed and the occasional globs of oil from distant passing tankers. The ocean's convergence with the land was as it had looked thousands, perhaps millions, of years ago, as long as it was viewed from a car doing sixty miles an hour on a road that hadn't existed at the beginning of the century.

Several miles north of Fort Lauderdale the Isuzu slowed and then turned into the driveway of one of several luxurious private homes with ocean views. Twin stone pillars marked the mouth of the driveway, and there was a chain-link gate across it that must have been opened when the Isuzu entered, but was now closed. The house itself was out of sight except for a long, red-tiled roof.

Carver parked in the shade of a grouping of date palms, made a note of the Isuzu's license plate number and the address of the house, then waited.

Not for long.

Twenty minutes later the Isuzu reappeared, bumping over the raised lip of the driveway, then turning south on 1A1, back the way it had come. The chesty little guy in the suit was smiling as he bounced in his seat and held onto the steering wheel with both hands. The little dog was on its hind legs, staring out the side window as if checking for road signs.

Carver started the Plymouth and fell in behind as the Isuzu built up speed, catching a glimpse of the gate gliding shut as he passed the driveway.

He leaned back in the Plymouth's upholstery, wondering where this was all leading and what it might mean. The miles slid by beneath the car's singing tires, as the ocean rolled on Carver's left and the wind caressed his bare elbow propped on the hard edge of the cranked-down window. The sun began to set, and a few oncoming cars had their headlights on. The Isuzu's lights winked on; the driver playing safe. Carver left the Plymouth's lights dark.

On Morning Star Lane, in a going-to-seed area of Fort Lauderdale, the Isuzu parked across the street from an old apartment building with brilliant red bougainvillea growing wild up its cracked stucco walls, draping down from some of the second-floor decorative wrought-iron balconies. There were yellow bug lights on each side of the entrance, but one of them was burned out and night moths, out early at dusk, circled the other one, now and then darting close, daring death.

The chesty little guy strode across the street and through the flitting, suicidal insects and disappeared through the doorway. He was walking the dog on a leash, and not carrying the briefcase. There was a transom over the old door, with an address lettered on its glass. Carver made a note of the number, beneath the address of the house on the coast. Then he limped through lengthening shadows over to the Isuzu and peered inside it.

No briefcase.

He stood for a while thinking about that, then returned to the Plymouth and drove back to his motel.

It would be too late to call Desoto at his office, but he might catch him at home.

AFTER BREAKFAST the next morning, Desoto called back with the information Carver had requested.

"You got a pencil, *amigo*?"

Carver said he did. He was lying on his back on the bed with his shoes off, the receiver in his left hand, his right hand with the pencil poised over the notebook propped against his upraised right thigh. While he waited for Desoto to talk, he listened to the ocean whispering beyond the shrill cries of gulls and children on the beach; it seemed to be commenting on life from offstage, cautioning with its old, old wisdom.

"The Isuzu's registered to one Roger Karl, with a *K*. The address listed's the one on Morning Star Lane."

Carver squinted at the pencil point gliding over the notepaper, finished writing, and said, "Anything on Karl?"

"He's got a sheet," Desoto said. "Did time for burglary back in the eighties, but that's not his specialty. He's really not much more than an errand runner, but a reliable one who can deliver cash or documents, and sometimes people, for his superiors. A fella like that, one who can be trusted, is valuable in that kind of world."

"A bagman," Carver said, remembering the leather briefcase that had arrived at the Cuban restaurant with Adam Beed, then had left with Roger Karl. Karl had delivered it to the house on the coast.

"That's what he is exactly," Desoto said. "Another interesting thing about him, he did the last part of his stretch behind walls when Adam Beed was there. They were in the same cell block, no doubt knew each other."

"Old school ties," Carver said.

"But sometimes the alumni turn on each other," Desoto said, "like people from Harvard."

Carver again saw Adam Beed walking from the house with the green roof and awnings, lugging the briefcase he later gave to Roger Karl to take to its primary destination. "Karl might be a drug mule," he said. "What he and Beed are involved in might have nothing to do with Solartown."

"Could be," Desoto agreed, "but you don't sound convinced."

"I'm not. Good bagmen are too savvy and valuable to use as mules, and at this stage of his career, Beed's not likely to be involved in illegal narcotics."

"This is Florida, *amigo*."

"We got Disney as well as the D.E.A.," Carver said. "What about the address on Langdon?"

"Single-family residence belonging to Mr. and Mrs. Sam Ribbling."

"No bell rings," Carver said.

"Ribbling works for Gheston Chemical, *amigo*. He was transferred to their New York office two months ago. The Langdon address is for sale and vacant."

"So it was nothing more than a drop point," Carver said, thinking that what was in the briefcase must be valuable for someone to take such a precaution. And where had the briefcase finally landed? Was the expensive house by the sea its final destination? "What about the house up on the coast?" he asked. "That one vacant and for sale, too?"

"Not at all. That one belongs to a Jamie Q. Sanchez. No sheet on him, no additional info. But if he lives in that area, he must have money, therefore clout. Therefore walk with great care, hey?"

"You know me," Carver said. "I'll even use a cane." He doodled in the margin next to his notes. Concentric circles. "How do you see it?" he asked.

"Obvious," Desoto said, "assuming that what you told me's on the mark. Adam Beed met Karl for breakfast, talked business, and got the address of the drop and the pickup time. Then he drove there and got the briefcase, gave it to Karl after dinner, and Karl delivered it to its destination."

"Which means the recipient doesn't want Beed to know his or her identity."

"Seems so, *amigo*. I'd call that prudent. You should watch and learn."

"Only Beed's not the type to stay in the dark. And if I could follow Karl to the house up the coast, so could Beed."

"Probably has," Desoto said. "He's nothing if not industrious."

Carver didn't have to speculate out loud about the rest. Once Beed learned the identity of the briefcase's recipient, he'd apply leverage, maybe physical force. He'd be a professional among amateurs, a fox among the hens. If he didn't have a major piece of the operation now, he soon would.

"You nod off, *amigo?*"

"I need to find out more about Jamie Sanchez."

"Thought you might. When you do, clue me in, hey?"

Carver said he would. Said good-bye to Desoto.

He'd reached for his cane and had just sat up and replaced the receiver when the door crashed open and a huge, shirtless man in blue bib overalls swaggered into the room.

23

THE SWEATY mountain in blue denim shut the door and was on Carver before he could think. This was no genial emissary from the World Wrestling Federation. A moist, thick arm almost casually brushed Carver off the bed and slammed him into the wall. Through his surprise, he saw that the man had ragged, short blond hair and tiny red-rimmed eyes. Carver knew the expression in those eyes. He'd first seen it years ago when a schoolmate had used lighter fluid to set fire to a kitten.

Carver wasn't a kitten. And he'd managed to stay on his feet and keep his grip on his cane. The huge man had muscle, but much of his bulk was fat. He'd be strong, but probably not quick, and without much wind. And so far he hadn't demonstrated much in the way of expertise. Crude hired help.

His thin lips were curled in a smile above his triple chin as he hitched up his crusty overalls and moved in on Carver again. As he came nearer, Carver could smell his stale sweat and what might have been gin on his breath.

"Gonna teach you a real hard lesson," he growled, in a voice that would have suited a bear roused from hibernation.

Carver jabbed the cane's tip into his stomach, but didn't make contact with anything other than blubber.

The huge man almost managed to snatch the cane, then he backed off a few awkward steps on his tree-trunk legs. He was wearing a conservative yellow tie with a tiny blue diamond pattern, the sort sometimes referred to as a "power tie." It was knotted loosely around his neck and tucked into the top of the overalls. On his feet were boat-size brown wing-tips with the laces untied and dangling for comfort, the leather tongues protruding as if desperate for water. Was this what investment brokers did on off days?

He came at Carver again, in a predictably straight line. Mistake. This time Carver jammed the cane's tip into his chest just below the sternum, catching bone as well as fat. The big man grunted and his fleshy face twisted in a brief mask of pain. But in an instant pain became cunning. He said, "Tell you, motherfucker, all you're doin' is makin' this rougher on yourself. Rougher'n it motherfuckin' has to be." He edged around where he could come at Carver from a different direction.

Carver scooted over into a corner, narrowing the man's angle of approach.

"Motherfucker," the big man said, momentarily stymied. Smiling widely, he stood motionless with his fists propped on his hips, his breath a little ragged now. No problem here, his expression suggested. He knew he had Carver on the defensive, so he'd have plenty of time to figure the best way to get to him. It was a puzzle that seemed to amuse him, total offense against a fixed target who'd be an interesting recipient of pain.

But Carver abruptly stepped away from the corner, settling his weight on his good leg as he lashed the cane across the huge man's forehead. The mountain was slow, all right. His hands had barely lifted off his hips when the solid walnut *thunk*ed against solid bone. When he did get his hands raised to his bleeding head, Carver jabbed the cane deep into his fleshy stomach, drawing it back quickly before the man could grab it. As the cruel mouth formed an O, and breath and gin-smell hissed out, the big hands instinctively dropped again and Carver took another unsteady step forward and swung the cane like a baseball bat. As it met the wide head he felt the vibration shoot up his arm and almost dropped the cane. The big man stumbled backward, stunned, bleeding heavily now from a gash in his temple. Carver lunged, this time using the cane as a sword, aiming at the sloppy yellow tic knot. The fleshy giant gasped as the tip speared into his throat.

"I'll kill you, motherfucker!" he said, his voice high and hoarse, even if still threatening. But now there was doubt in it; Carver was supposed to be afraid, supposed to buckle, but it wasn't working out that way.

The phone rang. It was near Carver. Keeping his good leg pressed against the side of the bed for support, he used his cane to knock the receiver off the hook.

"Somebody probably complained about the noise," he said. "Or maybe the smell."

The huge man's breathing hissed like a blacksmith's bellows in the hot, tiny room. "Motherfucker," he said again. Not much imagination, Carver decided. And apparently some kind of oedipal fixation.

"You should have brought a gun," Carver said, reading fear in the cruel blue eyes. He smiled. "Yeah, you definitely need a gun."

"I'll bring one next time, motherfucker," the man said. He showed no inclination to advance on Carver again.

"Somebody's probably calling nine-eleven right now," Carver said. "Why don't you hang around and see who shows up."

The agonized little eyes flickered with the knowledge that this might not be a bluff. Someone might well have complained about the noise, or heard the talk about guns over the phone, whose receiver was lying on the carpet with the line open. The law might swoop down on them like cavalry to the rescue.

It could all be true and both men knew it. The balance had shifted so noticeably that it seemed to have altered weight and gravity in the room. Carver's assailant backed toward the door, glaring fearfully, as if Carver might suddenly charge with the cane.

Well, Carver might; he felt like it. God, he felt like it!

But he knew it would be stupid. If the huge man ever got hold of him where they'd be fighting in close, grappling, he'd be in trouble.

"You're gonna be real sorry for this," the man said, oozing his bulk out the door. "You're a dead man, you are. Dead, dead, dead."

Carver smiled and said, "Motherfucker."

The huge man slammed the door hard enough to make a framed Norman Rockwell print drop from the wall. The one where the big ruddy cop is scolding the skinny, contrite boy for stealing apples.

Carver let out a long breath, then slumped down on the bed and picked up the receiver. Said, "Yes?"

"Housekeeping," a voice said. "You got plenty of towels?"

Carver said thanks, the towels were fine, and hung up.

Limp now in action's aftermath, he sat for a long, long time on the edge of the bed, leaning forward with his elbows on his knees, both hands cupped over the crook of his cane. Throbbing pain made him probe above his right ear. There was a lump there from when he'd struck the wall just after the huge man had entered the room. He realized he was miserably hot and sweat was pouring down his bare arms and dampening the thighs of his pants.

After drying off with a towel in the bathroom, he retrieved the notes he'd taken during his phone conversation with Desoto and made sure his keys hadn't dropped out of his pocket. Then he slipped his stockinged feet into his moccasins and hobbled squinting from the room into the bright and baking morning.

THE VESTIBULE of the cracked, often-patched stucco apartment building on Morning Star smelled faintly of frying bacon. Graffiti on the peeling walls informed Carver of all sorts of interesting things he could do with his own body. He scanned the mailboxes and saw Roger Karl's scrawled name above the slot for apartment 2E. There was an intercom system, but half the buttons were missing, including the one next to Karl's apartment number. Didn't matter, Carver discovered, because the door allowing access to the stairwell and halls was missing.

He set the tip of his cane down and climbed creaking wood stairs to the second floor, feeling the thick air get warmer as he rose. There was loose rubber matting on some of the steps; he made a mental note of that so he'd be careful if for some reason he had to take the stairs in a hurry on the way out. Walk with a cane and you had to plan ahead sometimes.

The scent of frying bacon was stronger on the second floor, nauseating him and making his head ache. The carpet here was worn in the center all the way through to the wood floor. A dirty window at the far end of the hall provided just enough illumination to make out the apartment letters painted large and bold and recently on the doors. From behind the nearest door came the faint sound of an infant screaming desperately. Carver limped down the alphabet and knocked on the door with the oversize black *E* painted on it like a "Sesame Street" graphic.

No answer.

A TV began playing loudly behind the door of *F* across the hall. "Here's what you've won!" a voice cried ecstatically.

Carver tried *E*'s door.

He won just like the contestant on television. The door swung open and he stepped inside fast. If Roger Karl was alert, it would be best to surprise him.

The apartment was hot and still and furnished with cast-off furniture, not with the decorator touch. Carver limped across the faded blue carpet toward a door leading to the kitchen. "Roger Karl?" he called, being polite before he wrung Karl's neck for siccing the menacing mountain in overalls on him.

No one answered.

He leaned on his cane and peered into the kitchen. There were some crumpled fast-food paper bags on the tiny Formica table, dishes in a rubber-coated pink drainer on the sink counter. A clock on the grease-stained wall above the stove said it was much later than it was. The clock probably had something there.

A yellowed coffee brewer sat on the table near the paper bags. It was plugged into the nearby wall socket, but there was no coffee in the glass pot other than a sludgelike residue from yesterday. If Karl had awakened here this morning, he'd eaten breakfast out.

Carver turned away from the kitchen and limped down a short hall off the living room. The bathroom was empty, not even a toothbrush. He looked in the medicine cabinet over the white pedestal washbasin. An empty aspirin bottle. A plastic disposable razor with a rusty blade that had been there so long it had left a mark on the glass shelf. There was a bar of soap on the washbasin. Carver ran his finger over it. Damp. Gummy, the way cheap soap got. A towel draped over the shower curtain rod was also damp. He looked into the tub and saw wet dark hair like a spider in a clump over the drain.

He backed out of the bathroom and shoved open the door that must lead to the bedroom, looked inside.

The bed was unmade. Crawling across the stained white sheet was the largest and blackest palmetto bug Carver had ever seen. He stepped the rest of the way into the bedroom. Two of the dresser drawers were half open, empty. He examined the other drawers. Also empty. When he opened the closet's sliding door, he found only a worn-out striped shirt on a wire hanger, a black sock wadded in a dusty corner. He felt around on the rough closet shelf and came up with an empty shoebox and a pornographic novel about two cheerleaders forced to spend their summer vacation on a farm. He placed both items back where he'd found them.

The overalled mountain must have reported his failure to deter Carver from the investigation, must have given some hint as to the difficulty he'd experienced at the motel. Roger Karl had moved out, and in a hurry, possibly on Adam Beed's orders. Beed wouldn't have sent an unskilled laborer like the mountain to work on Carver, and he wouldn't appreciate Roger Karl's having done so.

The rooms had the look of a furnished apartment, so clothes and a few personal possessions would be all Karl had to gather and pack. Carver glanced over at the bed and couldn't see the palmetto bug. It had probably crawled beneath the stained and wrinkled top sheet. Karl couldn't have been too upset about having to leave this place, cozy though it was.

Carver nosed around the apartment for another fifteen minutes, not knowing what he was seeking, not knowing if he'd recognize it if he found it. He tried to remember if he'd ever found a genuine clue of the sort stumbled upon in novels and movies: a matchbook cover from a nightclub, a dying message, a bloody handprint. He didn't think so. Well, a murder victim once.

This time, too.

Curled alongside the kitchen stove lay a dead brown and white beagle. It hadn't gone easily. Its body was contorted with final agony and its teeth were bared. There was fresh blood in its mouth; it hadn't been dead very long.

Carver saw something glittering in the partly eaten glob of dog food in a red plastic tray. He noticed an ice-cube grinder on the sink, the kind that prepares crushed ice for drinks. He went to it and found it contained the thick bottom of a drinking glass and some glistening shards like the ones in the dog food. Roger Karl had left in a hurry and fed his dog ground glass so he wouldn't have to bother with it. Or maybe Adam Beed had taken care of that for him.

Carver limped from the apartment and back out onto Morning Star, where he could breathe easier, where the cruel sun at least seemed to purify the air.

Leaning on the warm trunk of the Plymouth, he decided that if he ever found himself in a different occupation, he'd miss the job but not the people.

|24|

CARVER HAD taken the last Percodan. He found a drugstore and bought a bottle of extra-strength Tylenol. He stood just inside the door, looking out at the sun-drenched avenue, and managed to swallow two of the tablets without water. There. Maybe his head wouldn't explode.

Just swallowing the tablets seemed to lessen the throbbing ache behind his eyes. He touched a finger to the lump on the side of his head. It hadn't realized he'd taken medication and was as egglike and painful as ever. First Beed, then the giant in bib overalls. It sure put a strain on a body. It would have been a lot worse if the big man in overalls had been good enough at his work to leave Carver with more than a headache. New bruises on top of the old ones inflicted by Adam Beed might have taken decades to heal.

He was about to push open one of the glass doors and reluctantly step outside into the heat, when he noticed a line of sit-down phone booths near the hair care aisle along a side wall of the drugstore. He fished for and found the proper change in his pocket, then limped to the end booth, settled down on the hard oak seat, and phoned Desoto.

"I don't know anybody whose description fits your big friend in overalls," Desoto said, when Carver was finished telling him about the morning's events. "You want me to inquire?"

"No, I don't think it matters. He was cheap help, and he'd probably have less idea than I do why he was hired."

"You don't think Adam Beed sent him?"

"Beed would have come himself," Carver said, watching a pretty blonde in a white tennis outfit saunter down the aisle and study the hair spray display. "Or if he had hired some muscle, it would have been competent help."

"So you figure Roger Karl did the hiring on his own, eh, *amigo*?"

"That's how I see it. Then, when the job was botched and he knew I'd be coming for him, he told Beed about it. Beed instructed him to run, if Karl didn't bolt on his own." The blond woman bent low to pick up a pink can of hair spray with gold lettering. She had long, tan legs. The tennis outfit was stretched taut across her shapely hips and buttocks. Watching her, Carver thought of Beth even through the headache. True love? Or lust?

"Amigo?"

"I'm here." He kept his gaze on the woman as she walked away toward the registers. He suspected she knew he was watching, but she was used to men watching her.

Desoto said, "You do want me to ask around and see if I can get a line on Karl's whereabouts, right?"

"Him I'd like to see again," Carver said.

"Would you like to see Adam Beed again?"

"At the proper time."

"I can't imagine a proper time for that. His execution, maybe. But I'll keep you informed, you keep me informed, hey?"

"Your back and mine," Carver said.

Desoto was quiet for a moment, then said, "*Amigo*, maybe we should end this conversation we never had."

"I don't recall any conversation," Carver said. "But thanks just the same."

He hung up.

He knew what Desoto meant. It wasn't good for a police lieutenant to possess information about a parole violator and not take official action. Carver had placed Desoto in the position of betraying either professional ethics or personal friendship. Hardly fair. Carver felt rotten about it. On the other hand, it was Desoto who'd sent Hattie Evans to him. So Desoto had already committed himself to the personal code that at times overrode the restrictions of his job, that extended his neck to a length where his head might be lopped off. That was what made him a good cop and a better friend.

As Carver limped from the drugstore, he noticed the edge had been taken off his headache.

Then the heat struck him like a softly wrapped hammer, and he had to pause and lean on his cane. The headache was back with all its violent strength. He stood motionless for a few minutes before hobbling slowly to the car.

WHEN HE'D started the Plymouth, he switched on the air conditioner and aimed a vent directly at his face. The rush of frigid air chased away some of the dull throbbing in the front of his skull.

He drove around Lauderdale for a while, past the Big 'n' Yum, then the Cuban restaurant where Roger Karl had met Adam Beed last night. Where the briefcase had changed hands. As he cruised the sunny streets he watched for Karl's boxy little yellow Isuzu, but he never saw it.

He drove out to Jamie Sanchez's place on the ocean, but the

gate was closed, along with a more serious looking tall chain-link gate behind it. Possibly Roger Karl had phoned. Or Adam Beed, assuming he'd learned by now where Karl had delivered the briefcase. For whatever reason, security had been tightened. He glimpsed lithe, low forms gliding through the foliage. There were dogs roaming the grounds. A metal sign bolted to the fence declared the estate was protected by an alarm system and trespassers would be prosecuted.

If they survived, Carver thought.

As he idled for a moment near the entrance, a huge black Doberman materialized from the shadows and leapt snarling at the chain-link fence. A man with a flattened nose that had its cartilage removed, in the manner of a professional boxer's, also suddenly appeared near the gate and glared at Carver. He was wearing what appeared to be a chauffeur's uniform, complete with cap. His lips were writhing beneath the mushroom nose. Carver cranked down the window so he could hear.

". . . help you with something?" the man was almost shouting over the racket raised by the barking dog.

Carver said nothing.

The Doberman was joined by an identical twin. The barking was twice as boisterous.

"There's nobody at home here," the flat-nosed man said, still glaring fiercely at Carver. The dogs barked even louder and hurled themselves again and again at the fence, causing the chain link to rattle and bulge ominously. The metal NO TRES-PASSING sign flapped and *boing*ed each time the fence was hit by all that dog.

Concluding that he was probably unwelcome, Carver drove away. In the rearview mirror he saw the man in the chauffeur's uniform walk out beyond the gate and stand hands on hips, staring after him.

Carver decided he'd pretty much worn out his welcome all

the way around in the Fort Lauderdale area. After checking out of the motel, he turned the Plymouth in at the rental agency.

Then he treated himself to a couple more Tylenol tablets and drove the Olds to Solartown and beyond to the Warm Sands Motel.

25

THEY WERE in Carver's room, in Carver's bed, breaking the rules, maybe breaking the springs. Beth was sure no one had seen her come to his door, and Carver didn't argue with her. He knew her; she was going to come to him when she wanted to anyway. Besides, he wanted to believe her.

Still breathing hard, he lay beside her, watching a rivulet of sweat wend its way slowly down her bare breast, along her ribs, clinging to her. Her ragged breathing rasped in rhythm with his own.

"Love in the afternoon," she gasped. "Ain't it grand?"

Carver rotated his sweaty wrist to glance at his watch. The crystal was fogged, obscuring the numerals. Beth laughed. He craned his neck to see the clock on the table by the bed. Three o'clock.

Beth clutched the top of the sheet and used it to pat her face dry. "Got things to tell you," she said, breathing evenly now. It didn't take her long to recover from most things, to recharge her batteries.

"You just finished telling me some interesting things," Carver said. A car passed at a crawl outside in the parking lot, its tires crunching gravel with a sound like strings of tiny firecrackers exploding.

"I mean about what I learned on the Solartown reverse mortgage money. This *is* a business meeting, right?"

"The minutes are in my mind forever."

"Better'n that headache you said you had." She scratched her hip. "Hmph! We got rid of that sucker in a hurry."

She was right. He decided not to tell her the headache was threatening to return, hinting at heaviness and pain behind his left eye. Not that he didn't feel better in a lot of other respects. "So what'd you find out?"

She eased sideways on the bed, then reached out a long arm and grabbed the bulky attaché case she'd brought with her. After dragging the case near enough, she opened it and withdrew a yellow legal pad with tiny, neat handwriting on it.

"Near as I can tell," she said, "most of the money from the sales of reverse mortgage repossessions eventually goes into the Solartown, Inc. general cash fund. Immediately after the company reclaims a house, a small amount of ready cash is set aside to make whatever repairs are necessary and to maintain the property until it resells."

"Do the figures tally?" Carver asked, meshing his fingers behind his head and staring at the ceiling. There was a bright rectangular pattern of afternoon sun there; it didn't seem right to be looking at it while he was still perspiring from lovemaking. Beth could sure do things to a life.

"The numbers balance," she said.

Carver gave that some thought. What were numbers but somebody's information, good or bad? "Might somebody be cooking the books?"

"Always possible. You wanna check over the figures?"

"Later." He knew she'd already checked and double-checked. "How'd you manage to get that kinda information?"

"Some of it's public record. Some of it came by way of the custom software Jeff the computer whiz lent me. You feed it subject information, and it calculates various program passwords and file names the way it would chess moves. And Jeff would send me information via modem. What I did—"

"You or Jeff broke into Solartown's computer system," Carver interrupted.

"That's illegal. Hackers go to jail for doing it."

"Some do. Will Solartown be able to tell its data's been raided?"

She let the legal pad drop onto the floor. "Maybe. Depends what kinda safeguards they had built in. We mighta tripped some delayed alarms."

"If the company's into something illegitimate, it makes sense they'd have plenty of safeguards and alarms built into their computer system."

"Wouldn't argue that." She didn't seem particularly apprehensive.

He watched a small spider make its way across the ceiling to the edge of the bright rectangle of sunlight, then veer away toward the supposed security of dimness. "Any way for Solartown to trace who gained access?"

"Doubt it. Jeff's software has safeguards of its own."

"Microchip eavesdropping," Carver said. "I hate the age of the computer."

"It's like all progress, lover. You become part of it one way or the other, either by adapting or getting paved over." She propped herself up on one elbow and stared at him. Her large breasts were so firm they barely sagged sideways. She was no longer sweating or breathing hard. She said, "You feel like telling me about that lump on the side of your head?"

Carver told her everything that had happened over in Lauderdale.

As he finished, she was gazing at him intently. Was she going to offer sympathy? Kiss the warrior's wound?

"Just thought of something," she said, and rolled sideways away from him to sit on the edge of the bed. She bent down to reach her open attaché case, then swiveled on her bare rear end to sit cross-legged on the mattress with her back against the headboard. In her lap was her portable Toshiba computer.

Carver watched silently as she raised the lid, booted the system, and began working the keys. Within a few seconds her expression became that of a mystic gazing into a crystal ball that held all answers to all questions. Computers did that to people.

After a while she said, "Keller Pharmaceutical."

The name was barely familiar to Carver. "What about them?"

Instead of answering, she played the keyboard some more. The disk drive clucked and whirred softly, as if in pleasure.

At last she said, "Major-league pharmaceutical company. They're one of the suppliers for the Solartown Medical Center." Studying the glowing monitor, she looked disappointed. "I thought I remembered . . . wait a minute." Her long fingers danced gracefully over the gray keyboard. "Not Keller—Mercury Laboratories."

"They supply the medical center, too?"

"They don't supply; they're a much smaller company that does research and development for Keller Pharmaceutical. I came across them when I was following Solartown funds to various subcontractors and suppliers. When the recipients were publicly owned companies, I used accessible information to carry the trace several steps further, assuming they might be acting as money launderers."

"I think I've heard of Keller Pharmaceutical," Carver said.

"Sure, they're headquartered here in Florida and they're listed on the big board."

"You thought a company on the New York Stock Exchange might be laundering money from Solartown?"

"I can name you two big-board companies that launder drug money," she told him with a direct stare, "so why not money from con-job real estate repossessions? Or whatever else is going on here?"

"Why not indeed," Carver said.

"Anyway, Keller Pharmaceutical's annual report shows regular payments to a number of companies, including Mercury Laboratories."

"That unusual?" Carver asked.

"Nope. They fund several research laboratories. Here's what's interesting about Mercury." She swiveled the laptop computer so he could see the screen. The organizational chart of Mercury Laboratories was displayed there. "The president and chief executive officer was Dr. Jamie Sanchez."

Carver said, mostly to himself, "Same guy?"

"Figures to be. Mercury Laboratories is located in Fort Lauderdale."

"Figures to be," Carver agreed. He dragged the phone over and punched out Fort Lauderdale directory assistance. When he asked for the number of Dr. Sanchez and gave the address of the house where Roger Karl had left the briefcase, the operator informed him that Dr. Sanchez's number was unlisted. So the address was correct. Carver hung up and nodded.

"I'll do some checking around," Beth said, "make sure the two men really are one and the same. But I think we can proceed on the premise that they are."

"Dr. Sanchez is moving money through a bagman," Carver said, "for whatever reason."

"Might not be Solartown money, though. Or it might not

have anything to do with Keller Pharmaceutical. And who's the final recipient of whatever was in that briefcase if it went farther than Dr. Sanchez?"

"I don't know," Carver said. "What I do know is Roger Karl sure as hell didn't want me to find out. That's why he panicked and sent the giant in overalls to convince me I should forget about any more snooping."

Beth switched off her laptop and snapped the case closed. "Way I see it, Fred, you were hired to look into an old man's death, and now you're into something unrelated and plenty dangerous."

"Maybe not unrelated."

"Why would Solartown, Inc. or anybody else want to do away with an old gent like Jerome Evans? I just can't buy the idea it's Solartown trying to set up his widow so they can reclaim their property. What do you think, lover, there's oil under that house?"

He wished it could be that simple. Poke a stick in the ground, find a motive. "Maybe it has nothing to do with the property. Maybe Jerome found out something he shouldn't have known. And maybe somebody was afraid he'd told Maude Crane."

"If that's true—"

"Right," Carver said. "He might also have told his wife."

Beth frowned. "You best move that woman outa that house, Fred. Soon as enough time passes so it won't look so suspicious, Hattie's liable to wind up a suicide like Maude."

"If she'll leave," Carver said. "I doubt anyone ever ran her out of the classroom in her life."

"Huh?"

"Never mind. I'll talk to her."

"When?"

He rolled onto his side, reaching for his cane. "Now." His headache flared when he stood up.

Beth idly ran her hands across her bare midsection, up over her rigid nipples. She said, "A lot came outa this business meeting, don't you think?"

He didn't feel like crossing words with her; his head hurt.

"Not gonna answer, huh? Gonna play the strong silent guy in charge?"

He told her to wait exactly five minutes after he was gone before she left his room, and to be sure nobody saw her.

She told him to leave the shower running for her.

26

HATTIE EVANS sat with her hands clasped in her lap, her knees pressed tightly together, her haunches on the very edge of the sofa. Carver didn't think she looked persuadable.

He was right.

"Nothing you've said changes my mind," she told him. "I'm still not going anywhere. I refuse to leave my home. When you reach my age, certain possible consequences don't scare you, so you don't easily abandon what's dear to you."

"This house?"

"This *home*," she corrected.

"I had the impression you didn't even like living here."

"It doesn't matter where home is, Mr. Carver. Or how much you like it. What matters is that no one should be able to uproot you from the place where you've sunk roots and grown memories. That's very important. The concept of home becomes less portable as we grow older."

Carver shook his head. "You're stubborn, Hattie."

"You would know about stubborn, Mr. Carver."

Maybe she'd been talking some more to Desoto. Or to Beth. "The names I mentioned—Roger Karl, Dr. Jamie Sanchez—do you remember Jerome mentioning either of them?"

"Of course not. He had no reason."

Carver decided there was no way to get through to her on this issue. It reminded him of when he'd once tried to talk an unwilling octogenarian into a hearing aid. "I'm uneasy about you remaining in this house," he told her. "Or anywhere you can be easily located."

"You've made that clear. But there's no need for you to feel that way. Jerome didn't have any secret information, or he would have told me." A faint smile crossed her features like a shadow. "He could never keep anything from me."

"What about Maude Crane?" It was cruel, but he had to say it, had to convince her she might actually be in danger.

"That woman was no secret," she said, lifting her chin high.

"I mean, he might have told Maude what he knew, and that's the reason she's dead."

"The woman hanged herself."

"As far as we know."

She smiled tolerantly, as if he were a pupil who'd spelled "Albuquerque" wrong. "Believe me, Mr. Carver, Jerome wasn't the type of man to get involved in conspiracy or illegal money transfers. He was an old fool I happened to love too much, but I knew him. He might well have been killed because he possessed some dangerous knowledge. But if so, he didn't realize he had it."

"The people who killed him, and possibly Maude Crane, wouldn't know how much he understood, or who he might have talked to about it."

"Use your reasoning ability," she said sternly. "If what you say was true, I'd have been murdered by now."

"No, whoever killed Jerome and Maude would almost surely wait. A man dies, then his grief-stricken mistress hangs herself.

Okay, that's believable enough. But if his widow also commits suicide, or dies an even slightly suspicious accidental death, credulity is stretched and the law might investigate and find enough threads to weave a rope."

"So I'm not in any danger, even if your theory happens to be correct."

"I think you might be in danger. There's some indication the people involved in this don't always behave rationally. And who knows what they'll consider a reasonable amount of time?"

Hard resolution brightened her eyes. "Danger or not, Mr. Carver, I'm not leaving here to go into hiding like a fugitive. Regardless of what secret Jerome learned—if any—I'm not about to be chased from my home."

Carver placed both hands on his cane and stood up. "You've convinced me, Hattie. Will you help to put my mind at ease by promising you'll be careful to keep your doors and windows locked, and leave a light on if you go out at night?"

"I always do both those thing, Mr. Carver." She stood up and walked with him to the door. "Let me know if you need additional payment. I appreciate the job you're doing on this. You've gone much further than the police would have, I'm sure."

"I'm sure, too," Carver said. He opened the front door. "There's no need for further payment right now."

"I don't want you working on this investigation because you feel sorry for an old lady, Mr. Carver."

He grinned. "You're anything but an object of pity, Hattie."

She thought about what he'd said and smiled.

Instead of walking to his car, Carver crossed the green expanse of lawn to Val's house. He glanced over to make sure Hattie wasn't observing him, then punched the doorbell with his cane.

It took Val several minutes to come to the door. He was barefoot, wearing dark slacks and an unbuttoned white shirt. The shirt had widely spaced, intersecting creases, as if it had been recently bought and not yet washed and ironed. The house was dim behind Val, and he was squinting into the outside light in a way that made him look more than ever like a leprechaun.

Carver said, "Wake you up?"

"Yeah, but that's okay; I was gonna get up anyway. Just taking a little nap. Patrol again tonight." He stepped back. "Wanna come in? Hotter'n a whore in heat out there."

Carver hadn't heard that one, but then he hadn't spent months on Posse patrol on the mean streets of Solartown, as had Rathawk Two. He followed Val into the dim living room and watched him open the blinds enough to let in a bearable amount of light. It illuminated the dust.

"Wanna beer?" he asked Carver.

"Sure."

Val disappeared into the kitchen. While he was in there clattering around, Carver looked over the living room. It was laid out like Hattie's, with the door to the left of the picture window, door to the hall and kitchen directly opposite it. The wall-to-wall carpet was predictably green. The furniture was early American and functional; where there was upholstery, it was plaid. A wooden bookshelf contained a row of paperback espionage novels—which explained Val's knowledge of Russian assassination methods—and a statue of a horse, and a bowling trophy. Near a recliner the remote control for the console TV lay on the carpet, along with a scattering of what looked like popcorn. The fireplace had a small folding screen set up in front of its cavity, on which was a print of that famous painting of dogs playing poker. Carver thought the place could use a woman's touch.

Val had returned with two cans of Bud Light and caught Carver eyeballing the living room.

"Decor ain't for shit," Val said, handing Carver one of the beers, "but it's clean and comfortable."

"All you could reasonably require," Carver said. He wasn't

hypocritical enough to criticize Rathawk Two's taste in furnishings and accessories. He'd always liked that dog painting and sort of wished he owned one.

He took a sip of beer so cold it must have been within a few degrees of freezing. "Good," he said, licking foam from his upper lip. "I just came from next door."

Val sat in the recliner but didn't tilt it back. "So how's Hattie?"

"She's doing okay, but I'm a little worried about her. Maybe the Posse, and you in particular, could keep a watch on her house."

"Sure. She in some kinda danger?"

"I think so. She doesn't."

Val scratched his side beneath the unbuttoned shirt and chuckled. "That's Hattie for you."

"I figure maybe Jerome Evans knew something, and maybe he told Maude Crane—"

"And maybe somebody thinks he mighta told Hattie." Val finished Carver's sentence. "Anything I can do," he said, "I will."

Carver took another pull of beer. "When you're on patrol at night, you ever find yourself in the medical center?"

"Yep. Now and then we drive folks there when they're having some kinda problem that's serious but don't require an ambulance."

"It'd help me, and Hattie, if I had copies of their paperwork dealing with one of their suppliers, Keller Pharmaceutical."

Val leaned back and considered. His sleep-puffed eyes glanced in the direction of Hattie's house. He said, "You're asking a lot here, Carver."

"I know." He told Val why he needed the information.

"You dead sure this'll help Hattie?" Val asked.

"No, but it might."

"Helluva risk."

"Life's a helluva risk."

Val leaned back and pressed his cold Bud can to his forehead, rolling it slowly back and forth, mulling things over. Carver rooted for the power of true love.

"I'm on good terms with one of the volunteers there," Val said after a while. "She owes me a favor and she might have access to the files. I can ask her, anyways."

"When?"

"Tonight, I guess."

"You sure she can keep quiet about this?"

"No need to worry on that account. Be hell to pay if word ever got out. Even if the medical center didn't prosecute, she'd lose her job same as I'd lose mine with the Posse if either one of us came down with a loose tongue."

Neither man talked as they finished their beers. Maybe it was that remark about loose tongues.

What have I done? Carver wondered, as he left Val's cool, dim house and limped through the heat toward where the Olds was parked. His arms were already glistening with sweat, his grip on his cane slippery.

Had he placed two more senior citizens in harm's way for nothing?

Would he live to become a senior citizen?

|27|

ADAM BEED, wearing bib overalls, was driving a gigantic
threshing machine toward Carver, grinning, standing up at the
controls so he could look down and watch the blades snare and
dismember his prey. Carver was trying to run through the wheat
field with his cane, but he kept stumbling, falling, getting up
to look back in terror and see that the whirring blades were
closer. Beed raised his right hand and flailed the air with it,
holding something—a bell! Carver could hear it now above the
roar of the thresher's engine. He tripped and fell, struggled to
his feet. The bell . . .

Carver woke up sweating, snatched up the phone to quiet its
nerve-grating jangle. He peered at the ghostly red numerals of
the clock by the bed: three minutes past midnight. He'd been
asleep only a few hours.

"Carver? You there?"

Rathawk Two. "Somewhere," Carver mumbled, touching
the cool plastic receiver to his ear.

"This is Val. I wake you up?"

" 'S okay. You rescued me. Jesus, I hate farms!"

"Everybody does. You was up late filling out forms?"

Carver blinked his tired, dry eyes. Grimaced at the sandy feel of them. "What's going on, Val?"

"Rescued you, huh? Well, what I called about, I can't get Jane to help."

Insects were droning outside; the air conditioner kicked in and drowned them out with its watery hum. "Jane your contact at the medical center?"

"Yeah, and she tells me what I want's way too dangerous. She's scared. Mainly of Nurse Gorham. Shame a beautiful woman like that has to be such a sadistic hellcat."

"Shame," Carver agreed.

"Reminds me of a wolverine," Val said. "Wolverines are beautiful and cruel, kill other animals for no reason, just like we do sometimes."

"We?"

"Not you and me, people in general."

Carver slowly wiped his hand down his face. His palm came away slick with perspiration. "Friend Jane know where the files are kept?"

"Yeah. She agreed to help at first, told me all about the layout, before she got thinking too much and the fear set in. The main file room, patients' records an' all in folders, is on the first floor and's in constant use. But she says financial and some duplicate files are computerized and on the fourth floor, in a room down the hall from the main offices. After nine o'clock nobody belongs on that floor, so she'd have no excuse to go up there. Elevator doesn't even run up there after nine, and the door off the stairs is locked."

"You were a volunteer worker at the medical center," Carver said. "You got any idea of how to get around this?"

"If I had, I wouldn't have asked Jane's help. All I did when I worked there was escort released patients to the door in wheelchairs so nothing'd happen to them on the way out and the center wouldn't be sued."

"Does Jane have a key to the fourth-floor door?"

Val didn't say anything for a while. "I know what you're thinking, Carver."

Carver shifted his weight on the bed. The springs whined. "See if she'll unlock the door, that's all. Then she's out of it."

"Well, expect I can get her to do that. She does wanna help, and she'd only be away from her station for a few minutes."

"You near the medical center now?"

"Uh-huh. My unit's parked right outside."

It took Carver a moment to realize "unit" was Posse code for "car." Hoo-boy! "I'm driving over there," he said. "Leaving soon as I hang up. Meet me in the parking lot?"

"I'll meet you," Val said. He blew breath into the phone. "I'm thinking of Hattie."

"So am I," Carver said, and replaced the receiver.

He sat for a few seconds while the remnants of sleep faded from his mind completely, then he switched on the lamp and reached for his cane and his pants at the same time. Hurried to meet Rathawk Two.

HE PARKED on the street instead of in the medical center lot, then limped to where Val's Dodge Aries was squatting unevenly in an end slot near a white van. The night was hot and sticky. The lot was illuminated by overhead sodium lights that cast a sickly orange glow and made the dozen or so parked vehicles look as if they were coated with oil.

Carver opened the Dodge's door and slid in to sit alongside Val, resting his cane between his thighs. "Talk to Jane again?" he asked.

Val nodded, staring straight ahead at the medical center's brightly lit entrance. "There's a side door used by Maintenance she's left propped partly open so I can get into the building without being seen. Fire stairs are right there. I take 'em to the fourth floor, and that door's propped open, too. It locks automatically when it closes so it can only be opened from the inside, so once I'm on the fourth floor I can get out okay."

Carver was surprised. The power of love to inspire foolish deeds seemed to recognize no age limit. He said, "I'm going in, not you."

"I wanna help Hattie, I told you."

"I'm working for her, Val. This is my job. I need you to park a little closer to the building, watch the fourth-floor windows. If you see a light go on up there, honk twice then drive away. There's no need for you to get involved in this any more than is necessary."

Val said nothing, gnawing his lower lip and staring at the building. Nothing about the building changed.

"My way makes sense," Carver said.

"Yeah, I suppose."

"What about the file room door? That unlocked?"

"Jane says it's never locked. She don't know about the individual file cabinets or whatever's in there. She said the file room door's unmarked, but it's the last one on the left, at the very end of the hall."

Carver opened the car door. "Okay, I'm on my way."

"Anybody sees you on the lower floors," Val said, "try and look like you belong there."

"I'm good at that," Carver assured him.

"They see you on the fourth floor, get the hell away fast as you can." Val glanced at Carver's cane.

"It won't come to that," Carver said, trying to convince himself as well as Val.

He set the cane's tip outside the car and scooted out to stand up. After shutting the door as quietly as possible, he limped toward the service entrance Val had indicated. It was a small gray door that was barely noticeable in the shadows. His stomach felt hollow. His mouth was dry. He understood habitual, professional burglars; always had. When he reached for the doorknob the real apprehension set in and he began to enjoy himself.

H E W A S inside quickly, standing at the base of a dim stairway that led to a small concrete landing and another door. He picked up the small block of Styrofoam that had been used to prop open the outside door half an inch and stuck it in his pocket. It had a jagged end and seemed to have been broken off a solid form used to pack electronics or some other delicate product. Probably some sensitive medical paraphernalia. Hoping Jane had thought to deal with the door on the landing, he limped up the concrete steps.

That door was propped slightly open with a similar block of foam. Carver eased through and was on a small, square concrete landing. He craned his neck and could see up the zigzag, brightly lighted stairwell all the way to the fourth floor. Since he'd entered the building he'd seen no one, and presumably no one had seen him. His heart was pounding like a mad carpenter's hammer. Sweating coldly, he smiled and began to climb the stairs

The fourth-floor fire door was also propped open just wide enough to prevent the latch from catching. Carver edged it open wider and peered into darkness. From his hip pocket he drew the penlight he'd brought and switched it on. The narrow yellow beam jumped out at eye level, and he quickly brought it down to focus on the hall carpet. He wasn't sure if light could be seen through a window from down in the parking lot or street, but it was wise to minimize risk.

It was quiet in the dark hall. The antiseptic hospital smell from below had permeated the third floor. It was a scent Carver hated; it reminded him of pain and the death of people who'd been integral parts of his life. Some of them were people he'd despised; still, their passing more clearly defined his mortality and in his way he mourned them.

Holding the narrow yellow beam low, he limped along the hall. All the doors were closed. Most of them were lettered with doctors' names, or words like ADMINISTRATION or FINANCE. Carver recognized the door he'd passed through a few days ago to talk to the redheaded receptionist and Dr. Wynn. And Nurse Gorham, the beautiful Marquise de Sade, R.N.

As Val's friend Jane had said, the door at the end of the hall was unlettered. Carver turned its knob and pushed.

No give.

The door was locked.

He quickly made his way to the door that said ADMINISTRATION and tried it.

Ah! Unlocked.

He went inside and limped around behind the receptionist's desk, then began searching through the drawers.

He found everything but keys.

As he straightened up with a soft groan, something gleamed in the flitting penlight beam. He focused the light and saw a thick ring of keys dangling from the lock of a gray metal file cabinet. It looked like a complicated insect that had been surprised and frozen by the light on its climb up the steep wall of steel.

He smiled and wiped the damp back of his hand across his lips. The odds were good, with that many keys.

He went to them and pulled the file cabinet's key from the lock. Carrying the key ring, he limped back into the hall and down to the file room's locked door.

He counted carefully. The ninth key he tried opened the file room door. He played the penlight beam over the floor to make sure there were no obstacles, then entered.

There were no windows in the room, so he located the wall switch and flicked it upward.

Fluorescent tubes buzzed and flickered to life, then light flooded the room and Carver felt a rush of disappointment.

There were no file cabinets.

The room was only about ten feet square. There was a small gray metal table in its center, with an IBM computer on it, a box of disks, and some pens, pencils, and erasers. A gray folding chair was at one end of the table. There was some sort of cabinet that took up most of one wall and had louvered metal doors.

Carver opened one of the doors and saw a bank of small, square filing drawers. He slid one of the narrow drawers out on its casters.

It was lined with 3½-inch computer disks.

He cursed anew the age of the microchip. If anywhere in the medical center there were printouts of whatever was on the disks, he didn't have time to search for them.

He saw that the drawers were labeled alphabetically. When he pulled out the K drawer, he saw more disks. All of them were labeled in blue ink. Under K he found "Keller" and started to remove the file.

Then he decided someone might notice it was missing.

He limped over to the computer on the table, and the open box of disks. He got the Keller Pharmaceutical file from its drawer and laid it on the table next to a disk he drew from the box. Carefully he peeled the adhesive label from the Keller disk, then pressed it onto the other disk. Placed the substitute under K in the file drawer.

He remembered a "Deceased" heading in the file cabinet. Quickly he found Jerome Evans's file disk and substituted for it as he had the Keller disk.

He took the genuine disks with him as he made his way out of the building the same way he'd entered.

Still on an adrenaline high, he felt good when the night air hit him.

In fact, great.

"GET WHAT you wanted?" Val asked eagerly, when Carver was standing outside the Dodge.

"I think so. It's on disks."

"Computer disks, I guess you mean."

"Yeah. So it'll take a little time before I find out whatever there is to know."

"With the world all complicated the way it's gotten, you're gonna need a computer."

"I know somebody who's got one," Carver said. He looked at his car parked out on the street. "Right now, I need to get back to the Warm Sands and get some sleep."

"Was tonight worthwhile?" Val asked, as he hunched forward in his seat and started the Dodge's engine.

Carver said, "I'll let you know."

He watched as Val cranked up the window to hold in the air-conditioning, then drove slowly from the lot.

Carver limped toward the Olds, feeling the thickness of the humid night as if he were plodding underwater, the stolen disks heavy in his pocket.

Val was right. The world got more complicated every day. Somehow, while Carver wasn't paying attention, it had been turned into an electronic jungle.

Making it an ever more dangerous place for hunted and hunter.

28

CARVER STOOD leaning on his cane behind Beth, looking over her shoulder. They were in her room at the Warm Sands, breakfasting on stale doughnuts and coffee he'd brought from a quick-stop market down the highway, seeing what was on the Keller Pharmaceutical disk Carver had stolen last night. He was fully dressed, Beth was in panties and bra, seated like a supplicant at the room's tiny desk with her portable computer open and glowing like a god before her.

It had taken her only a few minutes to key up the information on the disk, which consisted mainly of Latin medical descriptions and columns of figures.

"Not much here but what looks like a record of orders, delivery dates, and payment amounts and dates," Beth said. The radio was on in the room, not very loud, rap music. The human voice was never meant to be a drum. He wished she'd turn that crap off.

He leaned closer and studied the orange-tinted screen. It

would take someone more knowledgeable than either of them to know what the listed drugs were for, what the prices and delivery dates meant. Maybe a CPA with a medical degree.

While he was leaning so near her, Carver decided to kiss Beth on the ear. He was bending farther forward to do that when he noticed one of the abbreviations on the computer screen: MCL

Beth shivered as he spoke less than an inch from her ear. "What do you make of that?" he asked. He pointed to the half-dozen identical abbreviations.

She rubbed her knuckle in her ear. "That your mind's not entirely on the job."

"I mean those sets of letters. They might stand for Mercury Laboratories."

"If they do," Beth said, "it appears some of the medical supplies were drop-shipped. Ordered and paid for through Keller Pharmaceutical but delivered direct from Mercury."

"Nothing necessarily unusual there," Carver said, "but it does isolate the Keller drugs that were developed by Mercury."

"Some of them, anyway," Beth said. "Other Mercury shipments might have reached the medical center by way of Keller."

Carver straightened up, leaning on his cane and still gazing at the computer screen. The names of the drugs, be they generic or commercial, meant nothing to him. But then he didn't read Latin. He took a bite of chocolate-iced cake doughnut, licked his fingers, and reached for his foam cup of coffee where it sat on the desk. He chewed, swallowed, sipped. Said, "Let's see what's on the Jerome Evans disk."

Beth changed disks and went through her ritual with the computer, mumbling under her breath about EXE commands and paths. It was a lingo Carver regarded as intelligible as Latin. A fly droned close to the computer. Without bothering to look directly at it, she managed to knock it across the room with a casual backhand flick, a blur of dark flesh and red fingernails. Maybe EXE stood for "exterminator."

She punched several keys in quick succession. The disk drive *whirr*ed and *clunk*ed softly, the screen flickered, and there was the information they sought.

The Jerome Evans file contained a plethora of information, from the date and time of his check-in at Emergency, to the date and time of his expiration written on what Beth called a scanner copy of the death certificate. From what Carver could make out, the autopsy revealed fatal damage to the heart. Jerome also had prostate cancer, but it was in the beginning stages and was in no way a factor in his death. As Hattie had told Carver, the official cause of her husband's death was listed as cardiac arrest. The trauma to the heart was effected by a massive blood clot that had moved into the aorta. There was Dr. Wynn's signature attesting to all of this.

"Know anything about heart attacks?" Carver asked.

Beth said, "I know enough to see what happened here. The heart had no way to pump blood out while it was still pulling blood in. It exploded."

He tried to imagine how that might have felt, acutely aware of the thumping of his own heart. What he felt was a pang of pity for Jerome Evans. Then a tickle of fear. It could happen to him. He decided he'd better pay more attention to his diet, cut down on fats and cholesterol. Definitely.

"Ready to move on?" Beth asked. She was watching his reflection in the mirror over the dresser but near the desk. He nodded and she scrolled the information on the screen.

The brief history of Jerome Evans's treatment at the medical center was there, from when he'd come in for his routine checkup, to when he'd been brought in two months later by ambulance on the day of his death. Readings from his blood sample workups (Carver noticed Jerome's cholesterol level had been only slightly higher than his own), a record of body temperature, reflex responses, and blood pressure readings.

Beth reached the end of the file. "Notice," she said, "there's no record of an electrocardiogram?"

"He was almost dead when they brought him in," Carver said.

"I meant from before then, from his physical examination. Heart's something they always check, 'specially in a man that age."

She was right, but that wasn't what interested Carver. "Something else is conspicuous by its absence," he said. "There's no record of medication."

"Digitalis," Beth said, scrolling up and pointing at the screen. "Day of his heart attack. Looks like massive, desperation doses."

"But that's it," Carver said. "Nothing else. Nothing earlier in relation to his routine physical. Wouldn't you say that was odd for a seventy-year-old patient? I mean, he wasn't given blood pressure pills or anything."

"This says he didn't have high blood pressure."

"Maybe not that, but you'd think he'd have some ailment. According to his file, the old guy was healthier than I am."

Beth smiled at him in the mirror. "Maybe you better enjoy life while you can."

"Will that thing print?" he asked, pointing to the computer with his cane.

"I don't have a printer with me, but there are places that rent them or charge to use them. I can probably scare one up."

"All I need," he said, "is a list of the drugs supplied directly from Mercury Labs."

"We can do that with paper and pencil," she said. She scrolled back to the beginning of the file, got some Warm Sands stationery and a ballpoint pen from the desk drawer, and jotted down the information Carver had requested. Her left hand worked the computer, her right hand worked the pen, while she glanced back and forth between screen and paper. Very dexterous, physically and mentally. He thought she was beautiful in her intensity.

When she was finished she handed him the product of low and high tech, and he folded it and slipped it in his shirt pocket.

"Gonna cross-check with Hattie?" she asked.

"That's the plan," Carver said. "I want to know if Jerome was on any medication." He thought again of his own cholesterol count; the doctor had cautioned him to cut down on fatty foods, mentioned something about too much bad cholesterol, not enough good, as if health were a question of ethics. "And if so, was it part of a drop shipment from Mercury? Hattie should be able to remember what he might have been taking. Could be she even still has the container, if he died before he'd emptied it. Trouble is, empty prescription bottles aren't the sort of keepsakes grieving widows tend to save."

Beth leaned back from the desk and looked up at him. "No, Fred, you're wrong about that."

He hoped so. He'd try to find out as soon as he finished his doughnut.

29

NINE O'CLOCK. Carver figured Hattie would be up and about by now. Probably she'd been awake for hours, watering plants, dusting, waxing, organizing her world so it had purpose, so she could continue to cope. Carver understood. Didn't he do the same sort of thing? Wasn't that his work, keeping the world orderly via something called justice?

When he phoned Hattie she told him she'd been awake since seven. "I've been up since six," he lied, not wanting to be topped, then told her why he'd called. She invited him to come right over to the house, if he had something he wanted to discuss in person. No sense burning up the phone line, she said, and she had things to do. And she hoped he'd be able to make sense, having been awake since six o'clock.

Carver smiled and hung up. He told Beth where he was going and asked what she had planned for the rest of the morning.

"Gonna modem those files to Jeff Mehling," she said, "and let him come up with an analysis that might tell us something more. Then I'm gonna crawl back in that bed and doze awhile. Recover from last night."

Six A.M. Carver couldn't argue with that one. "Will Mehling keep all this secret?"

"You can count on it. We've worked together before and he's been tight as a clam. I tell him, he'll delete everything from his system after we exchange information and he's had time to study it, maybe run some software on it."

"Tell him, then," Carver said. "And point out he's involved in the theft of confidential medical records."

She rose from her chair and leaned back, supporting herself with her buttocks against the desk, tall enough to be almost in a sitting position. She crossed her arms and smiled. "He'll know that, Fred. Not to worry, we're all thick as thieves."

"Thieves have been known to fall out."

"Not thieves like us, lover." She ran a finger along the inside of one of her bra straps, causing the cup to strain away and reveal a swell of breast highlighted with perspiration in the lamplight and glow from the computer screen. "Wanna come back to bed with me for a while?"

"Wanting and doing are two different things."

"Never noticed that about you, Fred, when you didn't have some kinda substitution in mind."

There was no point in trying to deal with this woman when she was in the mood to dogfight.

Carver walked to the window and parted the drapes a few inches, peered outside. Up near the other end of the parking lot a blond man and a blond woman were loading suitcases into the trunk of a car with one of those phony convertible tops that made no sense to Carver. It had a green license plate. He didn't know which state the plate represented, but it wasn't Florida.

He waited until the man and woman had gotten into their

ersatz convertible and departed. It was wise not to let anyone see him leave Beth's room, even an apparently vacationing couple from out of state.

The lot was deserted now in the thick morning sunlight. He nodded good-bye to Beth and slipped out the door. Heard her say, "Later, lover," as the latch clicked solidly behind him.

He twisted the knob both directions to make sure the door was locked.

The Olds was parked on the edge of the lot, in partial shade from a grouping of date palms. The hazed plastic rear window of the canvas top, the overlaying jagged shadows of the palm fronds, kept Carver from noticing until he was almost to the car that there was a figure on the passenger side of the front seat.

He stopped and planted his cane in loose gravel, feeling his adrenaline kick in as if he'd just downed a jolt of hundred-proof liquor. The Colt was in its belt holster beneath his untucked, baggy tropical shirt, multicolored flowers and birds of paradise on a black background. He touched its comforting bulk, keeping his thumb beneath the hem of the wild shirt so he could get the gun out in a hurry if necessary.

A breeze built up with a sound like a sigh and rattled the palm fronds overhead, causing the shadows to waver and making it even more difficult to see in through the Olds's back window. Carver moved forward, changing course slightly so he could approach the car from a different angle.

Through the clearer side window he saw that the figure in the Olds was familiar.

It took a few seconds for the penny to drop.

Roger Karl.

Carver raised his shirt enough for his hand to make contact with the checked butt of the Colt, limping closer to the car.

Karl didn't move. If he'd heard Carver's approach with the cane on the gravel, he gave no indication. He continued to sit slumped with his head down, as if he might be studying something in his lap.

A few feet from the Olds, Carver recognized the perfect stillness of his passenger, the subtle but chilling difference between the animate and inanimate. Roger Karl's category in Twenty Questions had changed from animal to mineral. Carver glanced quickly about and limped to the passenger-side door and opened it.

Karl sat with his knees apart and his ankles crossed. His head was bowed as if it had become unbearably heavy, his jaw slack. His hands were folded limply in his lap. The fingers were as pale as bone. His white shirt front and the lap of his pastel yellow slacks were crusted with blood, but there was very little blood on the seat, and only half a dozen flies were feasting on what had been Roger Karl; he'd been dead when he was placed in the car. His open mouth was filled with coagulated blood and his lips and chin were caked with darker dried blood. Despite the relaxed position of his body, there was agony and horror in his wide eyes and the pitiful twist of his brow. In his mouth, on his chin, even in the blood on his shirt, was a lumpy substance he'd vomited, and throughout the crusted scarlet-brown mess tiny glass splinters glinted like shards of diamond.

Carver had seen this before in Karl's kitchen, the dead dog by the stove. Not long ago, Roger Karl had been forced to eat hamburger laced with ground glass.

Gently closing the car door, Carver spat out the tainted, coppery taste in his mouth. He couldn't spit out the fear. He limped toward his room.

The door looked okay but he entered with the Colt drawn, prepared to use it, his senses buzzing.

But the room was empty, cool, deceptively calm and restful, as if nothing unusual had happened and there wasn't a dead bagman outside in Carver's car.

He went to the phone, pecked out the number of Beth's room, then told her what had happened and to stay where she was with her door locked.

Then he phoned Hattie Evans and told her he'd be late but didn't tell her why.

Then he placed the Colt in the back of a dresser drawer and called Desoto.

|30|

THE UNIFORMS arrived first, and in a hurry, two of them in a dusty Orlando patrol car with siren warbling and red and blue roof-bar lights winking feebly against the bright sun. Then an ambulance. No need for that. Then Desoto and a short, blond plainclothes cop Carver recognized as Captain Harvey Metzger. The captain had joined the department not long after Carver had been pensioned into civilian life, and he'd soon gained the kind of reputation Heinrich Himmler would have envied.

The uniforms had gotten the story from Carver, not too complicated as Carver told it, warming up for what he knew was coming. A morning surprise, a dead man in his car. Yes, he knew the man's identity. Roger Karl. Carver explained to them how he was investigating the death of Jerome Evans, and he'd seen Karl in Fort Lauderdale with a big man who'd beaten him—Carver—so he'd followed Karl to his apartment, gone there later to confront him, and found he'd left, and that was about all he knew concerning Karl until this morning.

He was running through this again but in greater detail for Desoto and Captain Metzger, when a blue Chevy with a SOLARTOWN POSSE bumper sticker drove into the lot and parked. An elderly guy in a green golf shirt, sagging Levi's, and white sneakers climbed out and talked to one of the uniforms.

As Carver watched, the old guy clenched his fists, jutted out his jaw, and looked righteous and angry. A murder, right here on the edge of Solartown and practically under the Posse's noses. He was as outraged as if an adult movie theater had opened up.

Everyone stopped talking as the police photographer and technicians stood back and Karl's body was removed from Carver's car and zipped into a plastic body bag. Even where they were standing fifty feet away, the ratchety sound of the zipper ripped through the air and gave Carver a chill.

"We're gonna have to keep your vehicle for a while," Metzger said to Carver. He was one of those military-erect short men who seemed to feel that every vertical inch was precious and stood as if suspended by a string attached to the top of his head. Hattie's counterpart in posture. His blue eyes were shrewd and ornery in his fortyish, pockmarked face. He had an underslung chin and an oversize, pointed nose that lent him a birdlike, predatory expression. "It'll be towed. You can ride with us into Orlando so we can get your statement officially."

Carver leaned on his cane and nodded, not feeling so good. Desoto, as always a fashion plate at the crime scene, stood with his hands in the pockets of his cream-colored suit and looked unconcerned yet thoughtful, like a leading man between takes on a movie shoot. Desoto was in a delicate position now, Carver knew, and it would be best not to bring up Adam Beed's name in connection with Karl's death. The only thing wrong with that, Carver reflected, slapping at a mosquito that had lit on his sweaty forearm, was that Beed was probably the killer.

Desoto glanced over at Carver, and Carver saw the message in his somber brown eyes: Metzger wouldn't understand. Well,

Desoto was doubtless right about that. Carver had heard plenty about Metzger. The little martinet captain wasn't the type to look lightly on a kink in investigative procedure, however well intentioned. In Metzger's book, the means justified the means.

After prudently holding his silence during the drive in to the city, Carver gave his statement in Desoto's office in the Municipal Justice Building. A tape was running, and Captain Metzger was standing at parade rest with his head tilted slightly to the side, listening to Carver as if trying to pick up something at a decibel level the recorder might miss.

Carver went into his highwire act for the police. He told them about being in Beth's room. They'd want to get her statement, but that was okay. She'd had experience in fencing with the law, in the useful art of deflecting the truth without exactly lying.

It was an art Carver was trying to practice now, as he sat in a chair before Desoto's desk, speaking naturally, knowing the sensitive microphone would get every word, every breath, occasionally answering a question from Metzger or Desoto, but for the most part relating in his own words his version of the morning and what had led up to it. Working without a net, carefully placing one word in front of another and trying not to fall.

As he spoke, he didn't look at Desoto, who sat impassively in his desk chair. The portable Sony on the windowsill, usually throbbing with soft Latin background music, was silent. Desoto's dark eyes were deep and concerned, seeing a future that might not be what he'd planned. Carver didn't so much mind being up against the wall with the police, but he hated having drawn Desoto into the mess.

So he did what so many of the best liars do—he told the truth, but selectively. What needed to be put into his story, he included, and accurately. He told the recorder about being hired by Hattie Evans, about probing into the matter of Jerome Evans's death, summoning Beth to come to Solartown to work with him, being beaten up. He left out identifying his assailant, and Desoto's involvement. He said that, while in Lauderdale, he'd seen the man who'd beaten him having breakfast with Roger Karl. Carver omitted Dr. Jamie Sanchez, talked about following Karl, being roughed up by the giant in bib overalls, then going to Karl's apartment on Morning Star and discovering Karl had left and taken his clothes with him. Cut to this morning then with Beth, but no mention of computers or stolen medical files, and then finding Karl's body in the Olds after leaving Beth's room at the Warm Sands.

There. That brought things up to date. He felt perversely proud. He'd wrapped up his statement without having lied, and without having mentioned the involvement of Val or Desoto.

"That's it, Mr. Carver?" Metzger asked. He didn't look or sound dubious. Which meant nothing.

"It," Carver said.

"A busy time for you."

"And painful."

Metzger pulled a pack of Salems from an inside pocket and touched the flame of a silver lighter to a filter-tip cigarette. As he clicked the hinged cap back down on the lighter, he held the pack out toward Carver.

Carver told him no thanks.

"You don't smoke?"

"A cigar now and then," Carver said.

"Explains the ashes in your car's ashtray."

Carver glanced at Desoto, who looked remotely amused. Metzger was putting on the clever act to show how futile it would be for Carver to lie. Scare him into thinking he might be in deep trouble if his statement didn't hold up.

"Anything at all in your statement you might want to change before we have it transcribed?" Metzger asked. "Before we hang it around your neck and make it yours forever, to float or to sink?" He said this with a straight face.

"No," Carver told him, "it's as accurate as my memory can make it."

"Good. I figured you'd be straight with us. You and Lieutenant Desoto know each other well, right?"

Carver said that was right. Desoto said nothing.

Metzger inhaled, exhaled. He held his cigarette between thumb and forefinger, with the burning end in toward his cupped palm, as if shielding the ember from the wind. "You were on the force here, I'm told. I don't remember you."

"It was before you came here," Carver said.

"I've been here almost five years."

"I've been gone five."

"Well, yeah, I recall now hearing about you and the shooting at that little market. Off-duty, too. A shitty thing to happen. You had the reputation of a good cop."

Carver said, "I was careless that time."

"That's how I saw it, too." Metzger nodded toward the cane leaning against Desoto's desk, pointing at it with the dead end of his cigarette. "You pulling disability for the leg?"

"Some."

"Good." Metzger walked over and extended his hand to Carver. "We appreciate your help, Mr. Carver. And we'll get finished with your vehicle soon as possible. You need transportation back to your motel?"

Carver grabbed his cane and stood up over it, shaking hands with Metzger in the same motion. "No, I'll pick up a rental car here in town."

"I'll phone when you can have the car back," Desoto said. "You gonna be out at the same motel?"

"For a while," Carver said.

Metzger said, "That'd be a good idea."

"You gonna let me know what you find?" Carver asked.

Metzger studied the glowing tip of his cigarette. "In the car, you mean?"

"Anywhere."

"If it concerns you."

"It'll concern me," Carver said. "A dead man sitting in my car, I see that as some sort of message."

"There's a possibility hasn't escaped us," Metzger said.

"You take care, *amigo*," Desoto said, trying to hurry Carver out the door before the fragile pane of professional civility was shattered. Metzger was one of those tightly wrapped types with a temper. Frustration became rage became explosion. The sequence was inevitable; the trick was not to be around him when he detonated.

Carver said he'd take care and limped from the office, wondering if Metzger's intense stare would leave burn marks on the back of his shirt.

HE PHONED before driving the rented Ford over to Desoto's condo that evening.

Desoto was wearing a blue sport shirt open at the collar, a gold neck chain, well-cut beige slacks, and beige loafers with silver-tipped tassels on them. His sleek black hair was impeccably combed as always, probably would be if you woke him up at three in the morning. He smiled but at the same time appeared sad as he invited Carver in.

The condo's living room had deep-red carpeting and drapes. The furniture was made up mostly of black leather or vinyl, stainless steel, high-gloss laminated wood. The carpeting and drapes were deep red. There was an expensive Fisher stereo on a wall shelf, softly pumping out somber Latin music. Not the kind of music Carver would want to listen to if he needed cheering up, but then he wasn't Desoto. Had never tangoed, and never would.

"Want a drink, *amigo*?" Desoto asked.

Carver said he didn't and settled into a black leather sling chair with gleaming steel arms. He noticed a painting on the wall behind the sofa, a watercolor of a black man strumming a guitar and grinning fiercely before a backdrop of dark and decrepit slum buildings. Desoto was heavily into art as well as women and Latin music, and, of course, catching the bad guys. Something about this painting drew and held the eye and the conscience. "New one, huh?" Carver said, pointing at it with his cane.

"Yeah. Fella out in California named Davis painted it. Guy with a lot of talent." Desoto's smile was one of pleasure and possessive pride now. "You really like it?"

"Sure. It's not the usual sort of thing I see around here." From where he sat, Carver could glimpse just a corner of the painting of a reclining nude woman in Desoto's bedroom. About half the prints or paintings Desoto had collected were nude studies. He had a weakness for women in the flesh and on canvas.

"You talk to Beth?" Desoto asked. How the man's mind worked.

"Just left her," Carver said. "Metzger and a uniform visited her at the motel, took her statement. She walked the line perfectly. Charmed Metzger, in fact."

"Nobody charms Metzger."

"Beth gave away nothing," Carver said, maybe too defensively. He knew Desoto had never become totally sold on Beth. Desoto couldn't completely overlook her background, her marriage to Roberto Gomez. The Chicago slums, then the cruel, posh life bought with Roberto's big-money drug dealing. Excitement and casual death in a sea of green. Not many escaped that world.

Desoto sat down on the sofa. He tugged upward on the crease of his pants so it wouldn't lose its sharpness, then crossed his legs. "This dead man in your car changes things, *amigo*."

"Certainly for him," Carver said.

Desoto didn't smile. "It's got to come out that I've known for some time where Adam Beed might be found, hey?"

"Maybe eventually," Carver said.

"Beed should be the prime suspect in Roger Karl's murder. I know that, but the rest of the department doesn't." Gold rings and a gold wristwatch glinted as he spread his hands palms up in a helpless gesture. "I'm a cop, *amigo*. This is a situation I can't let continue to exist. I mean, I realize I sent Hattie Evans to you, and nobody held a knife to my throat to get me to agree to the rest of it, but—"

"I understand," Carver interrupted. "I won't like seeing you getting mauled by Metzger for withholding evidence."

"And I won't like seeing you having to go into some other kind of work, *amigo*. I mean, we're both too good at what we do for that to be a positive thing."

Carver tapped the carpet soundlessly with the tip of his cane.

"You at all close to having the Jerome Evans death figured out?" Desoto asked.

"Can't be sure," Carver said honestly.

Desoto flicked real or imagined lint off his thigh, leaving his hand suspended in the air as if the lint might try to return. "Then it's a rough thing I have to do."

"Better tell Metzger tomorrow," Carver said, taking the load off Desoto. "You get clean soon as possible and you'll be in deep shit for a while, but your career will recover. You sit much longer on homicide evidence, you'll wind up suspended or worse."

"These are things I know," Desoto said.

Carver stood up, feeling the tip of the cane sink deep into plush carpet as he settled his weight over it. "Well, here we find ourselves."

"Two days from now, I'll tell Metzger everything I know," Desoto said in a level voice.

Carver let the idea bounce around his mind for a few seconds.

"A two-day delay could finish you with the department," he said. "You don't have to do that for me."

"I'm doing it for myself. Hoping for the best. Putting my faith in you as if you were the pope."

"It was your faith in me that got your soft parts caught in a vise," Carver pointed out.

Desoto gave his wide, white, movie-star smile, but his eyes were hard. Cop's eyes. "My, my. You afraid of such pressure, *amigo?*"

Carver limped across the soft carpet toward the door. "If they throw you off the force, don't ever consider being a psychologist."

"Two days, my friend. I'm afraid that's all I can give."

Carver said, "That's more than I asked for," and went out.

He didn't feel like the pope.

31

"JEROME WAS declared perfectly healthy at the medical center two months before his death," Hattie Evans said the next morning, seated across from Carver in her cool, neat living room. "Don't you remember, that's one of the reasons I hired you." The colorful oil painting on the wall behind the sofa where she sat was of a weeping clown against a black velvet background. Nothing like the art on Desoto's walls.

"Your neighbor Val once mentioned that Jerome didn't sleep well, roamed the house at night."

"That's true, but it's hardly a forewarning of a heart attack."

"Was he given any explanation or medication for his insomnia?"

A subtle light entered Hattie's eyes, and her back became even more rigid. Her posture gave the impression her spine might snap at any moment. Carver knew he'd struck a chord—just the sort of thing he was hired to do. It gave him satisfaction to see the light in Hattie's gaze become a gleam of respect, as if he'd finally earned his due from his tough fourth-grade teacher.

"It was a prescription drug to help him sleep," she said. "I remember now he came home after his physical examination carrying it in a little white paper sack."

"Do you know where he had the prescription filled?"

"Right at the medical center pharmacy," Hattie said.

"Because it was more convenient?"

"I suppose. Though usually we got our prescription medicine at Philip's Pharmacy in Orlando. They beat everyone's price on drugs. But their bags aren't white, like the one Jerome had that day. And he'd hardly have driven into Orlando after his physical examination."

"Remember the name of the medicine?"

"No. But I might recognize it if I heard it. It was liquid, in a little brown bottle I saw in the medicine chest or on Jerome's dresser where he kept it sometimes to take in the middle of the night without going in the bathroom and switching on lights."

Carver got the sheet of paper with the drugs the medical center had purchased direct from Mercury Laboratories listed on it and showed it to Hattie, leaning low over the sofa arm to see past her shoulder as she ran a finger down the list of Latin words and abbreviations.

"I can't be sure," she said, after several minutes. "Sorry, I simply can't."

Carver straightened up, folded the paper, and slipped it back into his shirt pocket.

"What we *could* do," she said, "is look at the bottle."

Carver let out a long breath and smiled. She'd beaten him to his next question. "You been toying with me, Hattie?"

"I wouldn't consider it, Mr. Carver. The dosage was small and Jerome didn't finish the bottle, and I don't recall throwing it away. It should still be somewhere around the house."

"I thought it might be something you'd hold on to," Carver told her, remembering what Beth had said about widows' sentimentalism.

She stared at him. "Why on earth would I do that? Do you think I'd get all misty-eyed over a bottle of medicine just because I'd associate it with Jerome?"

"No, I guess you wouldn't at that."

"I live for the present and future, Mr. Carver. One exists and the other will. The past no longer exists and never will again except in memory, and your profession must have taught you the reliability of that particular faculty."

"Let's test memory again," he suggested, "and see if you can find that prescription bottle."

She gazed sternly at him. "Wait here," she commanded brusquely, letting "young man" hang in the air. He watched her rise and stride erectly from the room. She'd easily be able to balance a book on her head as she walked. She was still constantly setting an example as she had for years in the classroom. Posture and penmanship had been important in her life and always would be.

He heard her rattling around the contents of the medicine chest. Then she left the bathroom and went into another room. The master bedroom, Carver assumed.

Silence for a long time.

She came back into the living room empty-handed.

"Memory fails again," she said in a distressed voice. She was frowning now, worried.

Carver laid his cane across his knees and smiled up at her. "The only thing in this world I never misplace is my cane."

She stood studying him. She didn't smile, but the etched worry lines in her face softened. "I understand that," she said. He thought she probably did.

He leaned forward in his chair, set the cane, and stood up.

"I'll keep searching," she told him. "I do think I'd remember if I threw away the bottle. And I'm sure it was more than half full. I can see it in my mind's eye, about five inches high with a black cap the medicine had left a crust around."

"Call me right away if you find it," he said. Then he scrawled Beth's room number on the back of one of his business cards. "If I'm not there to answer the phone, hang up and then call the motel again and ask for this extension. If you get Beth Jackson, tell her you've found the bottle."

Hattie nodded, took the card, and glanced at it before inserting it in a wide pocket of her paisley skirt.

"Don't forget to keep your doors and windows locked," Carver said as he was leaving.

She said, "I never really needed that advice. I've been locking the house securely since Jerome died."

As he was limping to his rented Ford, Carver glanced back and saw Val Green standing at his window. Standing guard over his ladylove, Carver figured. Val saw him and lifted a hand in greeting.

Carver waved back, climbed into the car, and drove away. Feeling better knowing Val was losing sleep over Hattie.

As he turned the corner off of Pelican Lane, a large gray Cadillac flashed past going the opposite direction on Golden Drive. He caught a glimpse of the driver. It might have been the infamous Nurse Gorham, but he couldn't be positive. He'd only seen her once before, that time he'd talked to Dr. Wynn at the medical center, and he couldn't trust his memory.

|32|

CARVER FOUND Philip's Pharmacy easily enough on Washington in downtown Orlando. It was a small shop, unusual in that it specialized in prescription and over-the-counter drugs rather than the general run of merchandise most drugstores now carried. No shoes or motor oil here. There was a kid behind the register up front, and a middle-age man in a white smock was working behind the counter in the back, near a display of vitamins and drugstore eyeglasses.

The cashier, a dumpy little girl about sixteen, looked at Carver as expectantly as a puppy when he entered the pharmacy. He smiled at her and limped back toward the prescription counter. She returned to pricing cartons of cigarettes, maintaining a profitable symbiotic relationship.

The guy behind the high, polished wood prescription counter was gray but fit looking, as if he exercised religiously and consumed scads of vitamins from the nearby display. He was wearing those half-glasses for reading and glancing knowledgeably at people over the frames, and, amazingly, they made him appear younger from a distance. Up close now, Carver saw that he was probably in his sixties. The plastic tag on his pristine white smock was curved up at the corners like a smile and said his name was Mark and he was a registered pharmacist. Carver wondered if that was how he was registered, simply "Mark."

"Help you?" he asked.

Carver figured most people could say yes. He saw that the front of the counter contained shelves of condoms and spermacides. "Hope so," he said. "I'm investigating something that involves prescription drugs. I need answers, so who better to ask than a pharmacist?"

"You're the police?" Mark asked, regarding Carver's question as rhetorical.

Carver told him he was private, which impressed Mark to the point where he didn't bother asking for any identification beyond Carver's plain white business card. Carver thought maybe he should get a wide-open eye, or maybe a figure in a trench coat engraved on his cards. He could go anywhere then.

He drew the list of Mercury Laboratory drugs from his pocket and laid it on the counter. "Which of these might be prescribed for insomnia?" he asked.

Mark studied the creased sheet of paper for a minute or so, while Carver listened to the distinctive double-clicking of the mechanical pricer on the cigarettes up by the register. Then Mark gazed wisely at Carver over the dark frames of his half-glasses. "Nothing on this list of drugs matches any prescription I've filled for insomnia."

Disappointment was heavy in Carver. "What might a doctor usually prescribe to help someone sleep?"

"Oh, a number of things. Seconal's a favorite."

Carver nudged the list with a finger. "You know what these all are for sure?"

"No, several of them I don't recognize." Mark adjusted the glasses on his narrow nose. "But if I had to guess which was a soporific, I'd choose this one." He pointed with a slender, manicured finger. "Luridus-X."

"Why's that?"

"I remember my Latin, 'Luridus' roughly translated could mean 'a deathlike state.' Possibly a description of sleep."

"What about the X?" Carver asked. *C-click! C-click!* went the pricer at the front of the pharmacy. The cashier still at it, getting to the cartons she'd missed.

Mark shrugged and adjusted his glasses again. "I couldn't say."

A tall woman basted to a glowing red approached the counter and asked, too late, which was the most effective sunscreen she could buy.

Carver thanked Mark and left him to his work.

After a stop at a McDonald's for scrambled eggs, sausage, and a biscuit, he drove the rented Ford back to the Warm Sands Motel.

BETH'S CAR was missing from the parking lot. Carver figured she must be out being a journalist. There was a battered black pickup truck parked in the only shade, so he parked the Ford in a slot near his room and climbed out. The sun had risen high enough to hit with brutality, and he felt perspiration break out on his back and seep into his shirt even as he limped the short distance to his door.

The first thing Carver saw when he entered the dim room was the message light on the phone blinking out a frenetic red signal. Maybe Hattie calling to say she'd located her husband's leftover medication.

It was cool in the room, but not cool enough. After turning the air-conditioner thermostat as far as it would go to the Cool side, Carver sat on the edge of the bed and punched out the number for the motel office.

Not Hattie. It was Desoto who'd left a message for Carver to call as soon as possible.

Carver rattled the cradle button until he got a dial tone, then phoned the Municipal Justice Building.

He was put through immediately to Desoto, who got right to business.

"Something you should know happened this morning down in Fort Lauderdale, *amigo*. A fella went to board his yacht at the dock of one of those ritzy houses backing up to the canals. Right away he noticed something big and blue floating facedown near the hull."

Fear formed a cold lump in Carver's stomach, then began to spread tentacles. He said, "Let me guess."

"No need to guess. Large man in blue bib overalls, dead."

"After a hearty meal of ground glass?"

"Not this time. His throat was slit. Lauderdale police think he was killed someplace else and dumped from a boat near where he was found."

"Lauderdale got any leads?"

"I know one they don't have."

Carver knew what he meant.

"There was an empty Crown Royal whiskey bottle floating near the victim. Beed's brand. If he's boozing heavily, he's hell walking, *amigo*."

"Maybe just purgatory," Carver said, trying to believe it. Big talk before the big game.

"Lauderdale's still talking to people living along the canal," Desoto said. "Another interesting thing, though, one of the dead man's arms is missing. Torn or hacked off at the shoulder in messy fashion."

Carver remembered the story about Adam Beed attacking a fellow inmate in Raiford. Desoto had said the victim's severed arm was never found.

"Bet I know what you're thinking, hey?"

"That business about Beed's first victim losing an arm," Carver said, "and the murder Beed's supposed to have done behind the walls. Is that on the level?"

"I don't know for sure," Desoto said. "I only repeated what I heard from more than one source. It was something I thought you should hear. After all, a missing arm . . . On one hand you can believe it, but on the other . . ."

"Okay," Carver interrupted. He was in no mood for the kind of black humor that kept cops sane.

"What this means," Desoto said, "is we got two homicides now, and they're connected."

The fear in Carver's bowels inched over to make room for the guilt. "If you have to go to Metzger now," he said, "I'll understand."

"I said two days, *amigo*."

"Forget the two days."

"No."

"I know there's more pressure on you now."

"More pressure on both of us," Desoto said.

Well, that was for sure.

After a long pause, Desoto said, "You got less to worry about from the big farmer, him being dead and disarmed and all. But from where I sit, Adam Beed looks twice as dangerous. You need to keep that in mind, *amigo*, watch your back all the time. You carrying?"

Carver absently touched the butt of the holstered Colt beneath his shirt. "Everybody in Florida's carrying."

"Gun World," Desoto said. "Stay careful, my friend."

Carver thanked him for the call and hung up.

Lifted the receiver again and called Hattie Evans.

"Luridus-X," he said. "Is that what Jerome was taking?"

"That does sound familiar," Hattie told him.

"It was on the list I showed you."

"But hearing it instead of reading it makes a difference.

Jerome might have mentioned it. But I can't be positive. I'll keep searching for the bottle."

"Let me know as soon as you find it."

"Mightn't the medical center still have a record of Jerome's medication?"

"Don't contact them," Carver said. "They might be part of the problem."

She didn't say anything for a while. Then: "When I collected my mail this morning, I found another note stating Jerome had been murdered. It looks just like the first one. Same color ink, same printing. Quite brief and to the point."

"What exactly does it say?"

"Simply 'Your husband was murdered. Don't give up.' "

"Was it in a stamped and postmarked envelope?"

"No, it wasn't even in an envelope. Just a piece of white notepaper folded once lengthwise."

"Save it," Carver said. "I'll want to look at it." But he was sure the note would be exactly as Hattie described and would offer little new. He said, "Has Beth Jackson been by to see you?"

"No. Should she have?"

"Not necessarily," Carver said. "I'm trying to locate her."

"You sound worried."

Carver realized that he'd asked about Beth because he *was* worried. She'd left no message saying where she was going, and the death of the man in bib overalls had him spooked. "I'm worried about you insisting on staying in that house, Hattie."

"If I weren't here, Mr. Carver, I could hardly be searching for Jerome's medication."

Faultless schoolmarm logic.

Carver cautioned her again to keep her doors locked, then hung up.

It was still warm in the room, and he felt overheated except for his forehead and bare forearms. They felt cool and were coated with perspiration.

Slumped on the edge of the mattress, his bad leg extended with its heel dug into the carpet, he called Beth's room.

After ten rings he hung up.

He told himself she was plenty capable of looking out for herself, and she was simply gone somewhere attending to business.

Nevertheless, he limped down to her room, stood in the merciless sun, and knocked on her door.

Got no reply.

He considered trying to slip the lock and examine the room for clues to her whereabouts, even fought an impulse to kick the door open and storm inside.

Then he turned his back on the door. Beth's unoccupied room would almost surely tell him nothing, and he'd be running the risk of being seen breaking in.

He wondered why he'd thought circumstances warranted that kind of drastic action.

The heat, he decided.

33

CARVER LIMPED back to his room and called Clive Jones at
the *Burrow* offices in Del Moray. Jones, who, as publisher and
editor of the pesky little newspaper, should know, assured
Carver that Beth's absence meant nothing ominous. While Beth
hadn't checked in with the paper that day, and Jones didn't
know precisely where she was or what she was doing, that
situation wasn't unusual. Once *Burrow* assigned a writer to a
story, complete freedom was allowed, and Beth was a top-notch
journalist who took full advantage of that freedom. Jones added
wryly that she might not have notified Carver of her intentions
or whereabouts because she thought he might disapprove.
Jones's tone implied his own disapproval of Carver interfering
with one of his ace journalists.

"That makes me feel loads better," Carver said. He liked the
free-spirited and altruistic Jones, but the man could be a pain
in the ass, like so many thoroughly candid people who casually
tossed around barbs of truth.

"I mean," Jones went on, "maybe she took time out to have

her nails done, or went shopping for a flannel nightgown. That sort of thing."

"Is that tact you're attempting?" Carver asked.

"Sure. I'm not always disarmingly blunt, only when I'm harassing crooked politicians and lesser liars. Fact is, Carver, Beth's smart and physically capable. I worry less about her out in the field, or in a hostile environment, than I do most of my other reporters." He waited a beat. "*Is* it a hostile environment?"

"Not unless you count murder."

"Huh?" Jones sounded interested enough to crawl through the phone line. "Who was murdered? Where and why? You mean the old guy, Jerome Evans? You manage to get proof?"

"Beth should be the one to tell you all that," Carver said, "if you can locate her. She's the journalist. So maybe you should try to find her."

"But I don't know where she is."

"So you mentioned." Carver believed him.

"Carver. Er, Fred—"

Carver gently hung up on Jones, not without pleasure.

He'd decided to stay out of Hattie's way while she searched for Jerome's medication, but he could drive into Solartown and cruise around, possibly see Beth's white LeBaron convertible parked somewhere. Maybe in the medical center lot.

It nagged him that maybe they hadn't been careful enough. He recalled the lipstick stain on Beth's Styrofoam coffee cup. Even something as trivial as that might have tipped Beed to the fact there was another player in the game.

Leaving the air-conditioner thermostat at its coldest setting, he limped out into the afternoon glare and crossed the parking lot to the Ford, feeling individual pieces of gravel probe through the heat-softened soles of his moccasins.

Less than a mile from the motel, he saw the motor home in his rearview mirror.

It moved in closer, its cumbersome, boxy shape casting a stark rectangular shadow that traveled beside it and somehow made it seem even more oversize and awkward. Carver glanced at the Ford's speedometer and saw the needle hovering near sixty, but the motor home was gaining. To the eye, it seemed not to be moving at all, too large and square to cut the wind on its inset, dwarfed tires, yet its image in the mirror was becoming larger.

He could see what kind it was now, a Winnebago. There were probably thousands of them roaming the Florida highways. Some canvas- and plastic-wrapped objects were lashed to the roof rack; the wind was whipping loose plastic like proud black pennants. Glare on the tinted windshield kept Carver from seeing the motor home's driver clearly, and the front passenger seat looked unoccupied.

A vacationing family in a rush, Carver thought. Running late to Disney World. Mickey Mouse waited for no man. Kept to his schedule. Had a wristwatch.

The Winnebago had closed to within fifty feet of the Ford, and he expected it to pull into the other lane and pass. The highway was flat and there were no other vehicles in sight.

The hulking vehicle picked up speed, but it didn't veer. It was almost on the Ford's rear bumper. Carver's eyes flicked to the speedometer needle, now at sixty-five. To the rearview mirror. So close was the motor home that it filled the mirror and he could see minor chips and dents in the dusty, bug-spotted cream surface of its flat, fiberglass snout.

He could hear it, too. Its engine didn't sound like that of other motor homes; above a ferocious roar it was emitting a throaty high-pitched whine, as if souped up and equipped with a turbocharger.

He glanced again at the smashed bugs on the wide surface. The motor home suddenly yowled and grew in the mirror. It was shocking to see something so ponderous move so quickly, fooling the eye in the way of a huge express locomotive. Carver's head snapped back as the Ford's rear bumper was crunched.

The Ford careened into the opposite lane. Carver panicked and yanked at the steering wheel, and the car rocked up on two wheels and squealed back directly in front of the Winnebago. He'd barely managed to wrap his perspiring hands around the slick plastic steering wheel when the Ford was slammed forward again. He was ready for the impact this time and mashed his foot down on the accelerator. The Ford was a production model Taurus, but it had guts. It squatted low and charged up to seventy-five miles an hour. Eighty. Ninety.

But the seemingly lumbering Winnebago hadn't lost an inch of ground after the Ford's initial burst of speed.

Ninety-five!

The Ford was battered again by the Winnebago's wide front bumper. Rubber screamed on the hot highway as the car rocked and fishtailed back into the left lane. Carver's cane clattered against the dashboard and dropped out of sight.

As he fought for control and tried to build up speed again, the motor home shot forward and was suddenly beside him, preventing him from steering back to the right side of the road.

Then the vast fiberglass surface began to edge toward him, as if to force him off the left shoulder where there was a drop of several feet. At this speed, he knew the car would flip. If the impact didn't kill him, whoever was driving the Winnebago would probably return and make sure his injuries were fatal. Another one-car Florida accident, and who could prove otherwise?

Something had come into view up ahead, wavering in the heat like a mirage.

A car—no, a truck! A big semi, speeding toward them in Carver's lane, directly at the Ford!

The Winnebago driver saw his opportunity; if he couldn't

force Carver off the road, he could hold him in the left lane where he'd be struck by the truck that was bearing down on them. The big motor home slowed slightly, then held absolutely steady with Carver's speed. The truck looked huge now through the windshield. The wail of its air horn came to Carver over the roar of engines, like the howl of a charging beast.

He caught a glimpse of a side curtain moving in the motor home as he slammed on the brakes and steered right, gripping the wheel tight enough to make his hands and arms ache.

The side of the Ford met the motor home, scraping against it as the Winnebago, with its greater bulk and momentum, couldn't reduce speed at the same rate. Its wide, flat surface was an advantage to Carver now, holding the brake-locked Ford to a straight course as long as he kept steady pressure against it, preventing the car from going into an uncontrollable skid and possibly rolling.

They traveled that way for several seconds, the Ford nestled against the side of the big motor home for perilous advantage, like a pilot fish snuggling up to a shark. When the speedometer needle had fallen to fifty, Carver abruptly yanked left on the steering wheel, away from the motor home.

The unexpected maneuver allowed the Ford to fall back. The massive grille of the truck seemed to fill the windshield as Carver willed himself to be patient until the rear bumper of the motor home had passed.

He rode the brake gently, praying his timing would be right, as the Winnebago's rear side window, then the back bumper, with a bicycle lashed above it, glided past with maddening slowness.

Then he jerked the steering wheel to the right, and the truck, its brakes and tires screaming and smoking, flashed past both motor home and car. The bucking and wind-rocked Ford hit the soft right shoulder, and its nose almost dropped off the embankment, but Carver braced with his stiff leg against the floor and wrestled the slippery steering wheel. Gave the brake pedal butterfly taps and brought the hood around to aim toward safety, amazed at the core of cool calm in the depths of his terror.

The Ford skidded to a halt broadside on the highway.

Carver put it in reverse, backed onto the shoulder, and watched the motor home disappearing in the distance. He cranked down the window, breathed in fresh air. The truck had stopped several hundred yards down the road and was on the shoulder. The driver, a husky man in a sleeveless black shirt, jeans, and boots, was jogging toward Carver, his beefy arms pumping as if he were punching a steadily backpedaling opponent.

Carver sat with his head bowed, both hands locked on the steering wheel, as the driver approached.

"What the fuck was that all about?" the man asked disbelievingly.

"Guy tried to force me off the road," Carver said. His voice was firm and controlled. Okay. Didn't sound like him, though.

"Sure as shit looked that way. You okay, buddy?"

Carver released his grip on the steering wheel, flexing his fingers to work the soreness from them. "All right far as I know. Safety belt kept me from bouncing around." He hit the seat-belt buckle release and leaned over, retrieving his cane from the floor. Then he climbed out of the car and stood unsteadily with his arm resting on the hot metal roof. He blinked and looked at the truck driver. The man was about forty, with thinning red hair and a seamed, sunburned face. There was a Confederate flag tattooed on his right forearm. "You catch a look at the motor home's license plate?" Carver asked.

"You serious? What I was tryin' to do was keep everybody alive."

Carver raised his cane in a kind of salute. "You did a helluva job."

"You're the one did the fancy drivin'," the trucker said. "You pull off that stunt-driver shit on purpose, or'd it just look that way?"

Carver said, "I don't know, myself. Little of both, I guess." He drew a long deep breath, something he keenly appreciated.

"Now you mention it," the driver said, "I don't think that motor home had a license plate. I can see it clear in my memory, you know?"

"I know," Carver said.

"Crazy fucker drivin' it mighta stole it, you think?"

"Probably." But Carver doubted it. The normally slow Winnebago had been specially modified for speed.

"Fucker drivin' like that, he musta been drunk."

"Very possible," Carver said.

The driver fished in a shirt pocket and came up with a restaurant receipt and a stubby yellow pencil. He jotted something on the receipt. "You talk to the law, your insurance company"—he pointed to the long scrapes on the Ford's right side—"and you call me if you need a witness. That asshole in the Winny's gonna kill somebody if he keeps up them games."

Carver thanked him, glanced at the receipt, and saw that the man had written "Tom Shannon" above a scrawled phone number.

"That thing still driveable?" Shannon asked, motioning toward the Ford.

Carver said he thought so. He climbed in and started the engine.

Tom Shannon grinned. "That a rental?"

" 'Fraid so."

"Bet they put you in some kinda pool. Tell you, though, they don't make a lotta cars would of taken that kinda damage and still run."

"Not even the Japanese," Carver said.

The driver stopped smiling. " 'Specially not the Japanese."

Carver decided not to argue.

He thanked Shannon again, then drove him down the road to where he'd left the truck with its big diesel engine still breathing black wisps of exhaust into the hot blue Florida sky.

After watching the truck disappear in the baking, shimmering distance, he waited until a string of cars came along traveling in the direction of Solartown. A white Plymouth, probably a rental. An old station wagon loaded with suitcases and kids. A green four-wheel-drive vehicle plastered with religious bumper stickers.

When the minicaravan had swished past, he jockeyed the Ford in a U-turn and fell in behind it. Speeded up and joined it.

He did fifty-five the rest of the way, drawing some comfort from the bumper stickers, flinching each time he passed a motor home traveling in the opposite direction.

|34|

WHEN CARVER entered his room at the Warm Sands, the phone was ringing. Each jangle was an explosion in the quiet, cool dimness.

He quickly closed the door and limped across the room, then lowered himself to sit on the edge of the bed as he lifted the receiver with his free hand.

Desoto.

"More good news?" Carver asked, keeping it light to assure himself the ground wasn't going to fall out from under him. He tried to convince himself this phone call couldn't be about Beth. He was being an alarmist about Beth. And there had been nothing in Desoto's voice to suggest tragedy.

"Information for you," Desoto said, "about the floater in Fort Lauderdale, the big man in bib overalls."

Carver breathed easier.

"Lauderdale law's done some digging," Desoto continued. "There was no identification on the body, but the F.B.I. had the guy's prints on file and a criminal history. His name was Otto

Fingerhut, and he did time in Georgia for aggravated assault and rape. Also did a stretch in Raiford for maiming a man in a tavern brawl."

"Same time in Raiford as when Adam Beed was there?"

"No, he was released six months before Beed was admitted. But he and Roger Karl could have met in prison. Karl did a brief stretch in Raiford for burglary. His and Fingerhut's sentences overlapped."

"Any address on Fingerhut?" Carver asked, wondering if he'd lived in Fort Lauderdale.

Desoto laughed softly. "Pinning down an address wasn't easy, *amigo*. Fingerhut's was a license plate number. He lived in a motor home."

The breeze from the air-conditioning was cold on Carver's back. "A Winnebago?"

"How'd you know?"

He told Desoto about the Winnebago almost running the rental Ford off the highway.

"Beed must have been behind the wheel," Desoto said. "Could be the Winnebago's where Fingerhut was killed, then he was driven to be dumped in the canal."

"That's how I see it," Carver said. "But why would Beed hold on to the motor home?"

"He might not be thinking too clearly these days," Desoto said. "His prints were on the empty whiskey bottle found near Fingerhut's body."

"So Metzger got an Adam Beed connection on his own. That puts even more pressure on you to tell him what you know."

"Two days means two days," Desoto said. He talked as if it were a two-dollar bet on a Dolphins game, instead of a ruined career and reputation.

"What if I told Metzger the facts?"

"It wouldn't mean the same, coming from you, *amigo*. You've got no choice in this."

"Neither of us does, then. It all comes down to bottles."

"Full of whiskey or ground up for hamburger additive," Desoto said. He didn't know about Luridus-X, and Carver saw no reason to tell him. Why burden him with more knowledge he should pass on to Metzger but wouldn't?

Carver thought about Adam Beed drinking heavily and what booze could do to reason. He'd never been an alcoholic—he was fairly sure—but he'd had his romance with the bottle, not long after his former wife Laura had left him and he'd been injured and pensioned out of the Orlando Police Department. "You think Beed's on a bender?" he asked.

"Not exactly," Desoto said. "But I think you've put him under strain, and cracks are appearing. He might be Superman but he's also an addict. Alcohol's working whatever dark magic it does on him. He's losing control."

"Maybe he's back on hard drugs."

"If he is, it's nothing that's mellowing him out. Alcohol's what he's used to these days, and it's all a beauty like him needs, which is why he's leaving a trail of empty bottles. The ones he forgets to grind up and feed someone, anyway. That makes him all the more deadly, *amigo*. You truly understand?"

"That was made fairly obvious to me out on the highway." Carver was under strain himself; he wasn't boozing, but the pressure was apparent in his voice, like tremors before a major quake.

"Okay, don't get testy. You get a read on the motor home's license number?"

"No plate," Carver said.

"No surprise there." Desoto clucked his tongue softly, probably in time to music seeping from his Sony. He often did that when he was thinking. "I'll relay what happened, get the state police on the lookout for the Winnebago. Meanwhile, don't forget to lock your door, hey?"

The same advice he'd given Hattie Evans, Carver thought.

Everybody was worried about Adam Beed. He was a whiskey-fueled nuclear missile with a faulty guidance system.

Carver assured Desoto he was playing it safe, then hung up. He wasn't surprised by Otto Fingerhut's background. Small-brained, smalltime thug linked with Roger Karl. Drunk or sober, a pro like Adam Beed would never have hired him. And to Beed, murdering Fingerhut was probably not much different from killing Karl's dog: the casual elimination of an inconvenience.

For the next few hours Carver lay quietly on the bed, gazing at the ceiling and going over the facts of the case in his mind. He chose not to commit them to paper; he'd found that by doing so he lost a certain fluidity of thought. Usually this kind of thing required going outside the lines or off the game board, a different perspective that revealed what had happened in a different light and scale. He didn't want to block any avenues.

Where he went was down the road to sleep.

IT WAS getting dark when he woke up. He phoned Beth's room and got no answer.

His stomach growled and he realized he hadn't eaten since breakfast. He stood up and adjusted his clothes, went into the bathroom and smoothed the hair above his ears, then limped down to the Seagrill and had a salad, tuna steak, and two draft beers before returning to his room.

After a while he called a doctor he knew in Orlando, a man with the unlikely name of Malarky, and asked him about the list of Mercury Laboratories drugs. He got the same answer Mark had given him at Philip's Pharmacy. Luridus-X was the wild card. The doctor gave Carver the name of a medical lab that would do reasonably fast analysis, and suggested Carver use him as a reference.

Carver hoped he'd have the chance.

About ten o'clock there was a soft knock on the door.

He picked up the Colt and tucked it in his belt, safety off, then went to the door and asked who was there.

Beth called in that it was room service.

He opened the door and she strode in, wearing lightweight yellow slacks and a white sleeveless blouse, tall and carrying herself like royalty. Her air of nobility was more than height and posture; it was an attitude that seemed to be genetic. She might have been born in the slums of Chicago, but every gesture and glance suggested the lineage of queens.

"Where've you been?" he asked, realizing immediately that he sounded like a disapproving father grilling a wayward teen. Hell with it; he couldn't help it.

"Spent much of the day doing a follow-up interview with Brad Faravelli, then had dinner with a source."

"Source of what?"

"You sound aggravated, and I notice you're carrying a gun. Something wrong, lover?"

"I was worried about you, that's all."

She didn't seem sympathetic. "I don't like it when people worry about me."

He'd known it, but the concern had crept in.

"You like people worrying over you, Fred?" She was pressing, grinning.

He walked to the desk and laid the gun on it, catching a whiff of her perfume. It was subtle yet forceful, as if derived from some sort of flower that choked off weeds.

"What'd you get out of the Faravelli interview?" he asked, all business. Still irritated, though.

"Reinforcement of my notion that he's a straight arrow and the Solartown money flows in proper channels. Also, he's more than a little interested in me." She winked.

"Maybe he wants to sell you a house."

"Bastard!" She laughed and tackled him, knocking him back on the bed. His cane caught on the edge of the mattress and fell to the floor. "He's rumored to have a mistress, a real humdinger beauty-queen type. Anyway, I said he was interested in me, not vice versa. But speaking of vice . . ." She was lying full length on top of Carver, attempting to work a hand between their bodies to unzip his fly.

He pretended that he was trying to cast her away, heard the bedside table with the lamp and phone on it hit the floor as she thrashed around for leverage. Giggling, she eased to the center of the mattress and let him work his way on top of her.

"How long have you had this libido problem?" he asked. He kissed her on the lips. She kissed back hard, probing with her tongue, then pulled away. Not amused now. Her dark eyes were misty, serious, pulling him toward the center of the earth.

She said, "Whatever my problem is, it can be solved."

He raised himself up on one elbow and unbuttoned her blouse, knowing from wrestling with her she wasn't wearing a bra. He felt her hands working surely at the button to his fly. The zipper. He kissed her nipples, then her lips, and breath rushed from her and she helped him with the bottom buttons on her blouse, with his shirt, his briefs, undressing him and herself in a mad flurry of urgency. A button popped airborne and bounced off his bare back. The bedsprings squealed and the headboard crashed against the wall.

He said, "This hurricane season?"

She said, "It is for you."

When he'd entered her and her long legs were wrapped around him, he said, "I wasn't actually worried, but Christ, it's good to see you!"

35

A BRILLIANT sunbeam lanced through the part in the drapes and lay in a gauzy strip of light across Carver's eyes. He opened his right eye, closed it immediately, then groaned and rolled over in bed. He could feel the warm sunbeam like a weight on his bare shoulder and arm.

He'd gone to sleep within seconds after Beth had left his bed and returned to her room last night. She sometimes had that effect on him. He wondered if Brad Faravelli had earlier that day laid a foundation of arousal in her, then he mentally kicked himself for considering such a thing. He didn't like to think of himself as a male chauvinist, but he knew that at times he must be, and he was working on the problem. Beth was helping him.

Realizing by the amount of light in the room that it must be later than he wanted it to be, he braved the malicious sunbeam again by rolling back on his left side to peer at the clock.

No clock.

No phone.

No bedside table.

Huh?

Then he remembered hearing Beth's leg or arm knock the table over as they'd wrestled last night like possessed teenagers on the bed. Some foreplay, that turned over furniture. With Beth, sometimes the earth moved even before penetration.

He scooted sideways on the bed, moving completely out from beneath the sheet and realizing that it was cool in the room; the air conditioner was still on high.

There was the table on the floor, all right, along with what had been on it.

Carver reached out and turned the clock around, then right side up: 9:15. He didn't like to stay in bed past eight, no matter what time he'd gone to sleep. Made him feel brain-dead the rest of the morning.

He grabbed the table by a leg and drew it nearer, then used both hands to stand it upright. Placed the clock on it, then the white plastic phone base. Reeled in the receiver, resisting like a hooked fish on its springy, coiled cord, and dropped it into its cradle.

Instantly the phone rang and Carver jumped.

When it began its second ring a bolt of pain shot through his head, and he snatched up the receiver and held its cool hardness to his ear.

Beth's voice said, "Fred?"

"Yeah." God! What a taste in his mouth!

"Remember me from last night?"

"Vague recollection."

"Hattie Evans just phoned my room, lover. She said she'd been trying to call you but only got a busy signal."

"You knocked the receiver off the phone last night," Carver said. "Knocked the whole damned table and contents over. I just woke up and put everything back together."

"Whatever. Thing is, Hattie said for me to tell you she found her husband's prescription bottle."

Carver came all the way alert and sat up. His bare toe touched his cane where it had fallen on the floor. "She say it was Luridus-X?"

"Didn't get into that."

"I'm going to drive over to her place and get the bottle, then take it into Orlando for analysis. Wanna come with me?"

"Sure, but I'm still in bed."

Where did she think *he* was?

"So meet me at the lab in Orlando in about an hour. Just a second. Hold on." He'd spotted the memo pad that had been next to the phone on the floor, and scooted off the bed and down to a sitting position on the carpet. After straightening out the pad's kinked pages, he found the analysis lab's address and gave it to Beth.

"Got it," she said. He knew that with her memory she never had to write down addresses or phone numbers. "See you there in an hour, Fred, and we can have some breakfast while we wait for test results."

He hung up, hoping she was right and the lab would provide answers about Luridus-X that quickly. Probably they were computerized and could do it. God bless microchips.

Using the mattress and his cane for support, he stood up and waited a few seconds for the room to level out. Then he hurried into the bathroom to step in and out of the shower before getting dressed and leaving for Hattie's house.

SHE'D SEEN him drive up and was waiting for him with the door open.

Hattie was wearing a belted dress that emphasized her waspish midsection and schoolteacher posture. The dress was made of some kind of soft, crinkly material and was white with thin pastel stripes of various colors that gave it a fresh, crisp look that suited her personality. Her perfume was an elusive hint of roses in the warm morning. She was smiling with satisfaction and a kind of eagerness, as if this might be the end of the semester and exam day. In a way, that was the situation.

"I finally found it in here," she said, leading Carver to the kitchen. The tiles and appliances were gleaming. There was half a pot of coffee in the Braun brewer, permeating the kitchen with an aroma that ordinarily would have made Carver hungry for breakfast. Not this morning.

Hattie opened a cabinet that contained a rack of small spice containers in front and several wine and liquor bottles in back. "It was in with the spices, where I must have placed it by mistake after Jerome left it here in the kitchen. We used this cabinet for nothing other than spices and seldom-served beverages like hard liquor and mixing ingredients. I haven't had much company or done any fancy cooking for quite a while, so I hardly ever looked in this cabinet. I don't remember opening the door since Jerome passed, actually. Anyway, I glanced in here this morning without any real hope of finding the medication, and there it was next to the anise."

"Where is it now?" Carver asked. He was eager to get to the lab in Orlando, anxious for answers.

She reached into a pocket in her dress skirt and handed him a small brown plastic bottle about the size of some of the spice bottles. Only this one had a medical center pharmacy prescription label fastened to it with clear cellophane tape. It was half full of a syrupy liquid that appeared quite dark, even taking into account the color of the bottle.

Carver held the bottle up and squinted at the scrawled lettering on the label. Nowhere did it seem to read "Luridus-X" but the directions were for Jerome to take one half-teaspoonful before bedtime if having difficulty sleeping.

"Sure this is it?" Carver asked.

Hattie said, "It's not the kind of thing I'd be unsure of,

Mr. Carver, or I wouldn't have phoned you or your, uh, associate."

Carver slipped the bottle in his pocket and told Hattie he was driving it into Orlando for analysis; he'd call her as soon as he learned what it contained.

Her eyes were bright and grimly determined as she said, "We're truly going to discover some things about Jerome's death now, aren't we, Mr. Carver?"

"One way or the other." He told her he'd find his own way out, but she followed him as he limped back into the living room and toward the door.

When he dug the cane's tip into the carpet and stopped abruptly, she bumped into him.

"Something the matter?" she asked.

"That," Carver said. He pointed with his cane at the sun-washed view out the living-room window.

A Winnebago motor home was parked across the street, and Adam Beed had climbed out and was buttoning his dark suit coat. He was staring at Hattie's house with a nasty little smile Carver had seen before.

Carver told Hattie who he was.

She stared out the window and stood even more erect, jutting out her chin. "Leave by the back door, Mr. Carver," she said firmly. "Make it to your car and deliver that bottle to the police or the laboratory in Orlando."

Carver watched Adam Beed stride toward the house. He was carrying an attaché case and looked like a prosperous, muscular insurance agent on his way to bore prospective clients. But he wasn't that at all.

"You're my employee, Mr. Carver, so please obey my instructions this instant."

He didn't move.

"You're being recalcitrant."

"I won't leave you alone," he said. "I'm going into the kitchen. If Beed asks about me, tell him I left fifteen minutes ago with Lieutenant Desoto, in Desoto's car."

She looked up at him with fear in her eyes, but also resolve. Carver thought she was about to speak, but she remained silent.

He limped to the kitchen and got busy, and within seconds heard the door chimes pealing like alarm bells.

36

FROM WHERE he sat at the kitchen table, Carver heard the chimes sound two more times. Hattie was in no rush to go to the front door.

Then he heard the door open, Beed's voice from out on the porch. Carver couldn't understand what he was saying, but his tone was amicable.

"He isn't here, I'm afraid," Hattie said. "He left with Lieutenant Desoto ten or fifteen minutes ago. Should I—"

There was the sound of a slap.

"How dare—" Another slap.

The front door closing.

Silence.

Carver gripped his cane and fought the impulse to get up and go into the living room. He hadn't expected Beed to become violent so quickly; if he'd been boozing as heavily as Desoto suspected, he might be on the very edge. Carver had handled it wrong. He knew that now but it was too late; he had to follow the course he'd set.

"I assume Mr. Carver's in the house," Beed said loudly in the living room.

"I told you—"

"I know," Beed interrupted Hattie. At least he didn't slap her this time. "Carver, you hear me?"

Carver held his silence. He'd screwed up about as much as fate would allow.

He heard movement in the living room, footsteps going away, then coming nearer. He drew the Colt from its holster and laid it on the table with his fingertips resting lightly on it. He hadn't wanted to use it, but he thought now there might be no choice. He'd used the gun before and knew he could do it.

Adam Beed appeared in the kitchen doorway. He was holding an AK-47 automatic weapon in his right hand. His thick left arm was clamped around Hattie. The left side of her jaw was ballooned out and her eyes were teared with rage and fear. The automatic's sleek blue barrel wasn't aimed at Carver. It was digging into Hattie's ribs.

"Ah, here's where you've been keeping yourself," Beed said, as if making small talk at a party. So neatly and conservatively dressed—blue suit, white shirt, red tie—and holding gun and hostage, he looked like a political fund raiser who'd gone too far. He was grinning but there was a tic in the parchmentlike flesh beneath his right eye. He appeared pale, strung out, and dangerous. A wave of fear hit Carver, and he waited until he had control before answering.

"What caused you to drop by?" he asked. He was pleased that his voice remained level and conversational. He hadn't removed his fingertips from the gun, but he knew he couldn't use it while Beed had Hattie.

"The social butterfly in me, I guess. Why didn't you say something when I called your name?"

"That old maxim, 'If you don't have anything nice to say about somebody . . .' "

Beed nodded toward the Colt. "I'd like that gun for my collection."

"I don't want to sell it."

"No, but I'm sure you'll give it away rather than see old lady all over the walls. Drop it on the floor and slide it over here with your foot."

Carver obeyed.

Beed released Hattie as he stooped gracefully and picked up the gun. He stuck it in his belt inside his suit coat and came all the way into the room. Hattie edged over to stand near Carver. She seemed calm but for a faint quivering in the fingers of her hand near Carver's cheek.

Beed's glance traveled around the kitchen. "Another thing I want," he said, "is a small brown bottle."

Carver said, "I'll just bet."

The flesh beneath Beed's eye danced again and he leveled the automatic at Carver. "The old bitch here's all I need to get that bottle. Something you should keep in mind."

"Another thing to keep in mind is that if I tell you where it is, you'll kill us both."

"Definitely. Gonna kill you both either way and it doesn't matter if we all know it. You two fall on the debit side of the ledger, and there's nothing I enjoy more than balancing the books."

"The way you subtracted Roger Karl and Otto Fingerhut?"

Beed shrugged. "There are layoffs in every business."

A sound from outside caught his attention. Carver hadn't heard it.

Now he did hear something, the slam of a car door.

"Let's go into the living room," Beed said, like a considerate host trying to put his guests at ease.

Carver stood up and limped after Hattie. Beed followed with the automatic, an unwanted, menacing shadow.

Through the living-room window Carver saw a gray Cadillac parked behind the Winnebago. Nurse Monica Gorham and an extremely thin Latin man were walking up Hattie's driveway toward the house. The man was wearing a dark pinstripe suit even spiffier than Beed's. Nurse Gorham was dressed in a severe gray business suit with pale stockings and white high heels beneath its modest-length skirt. Everyone other than Carver and Hattie was dressed for a board of directors' meeting.

Keeping the gun trained on Carver, Beed opened the front door to admit them.

Inside, Nurse Gorham gazed at Carver and Hattie with remote curiosity, as if they might be objects in an aquarium.

The Latino barely glanced at them. He had a smooth complexion and was almost feminine looking, naturally dark around the eyes as if he wore makeup. It took a second glance to see that he was probably in his forties. He gave the impression this was all distasteful and he'd rather be someplace else. Well, so would Carver. Philadelphia, even.

Carver guessed and said, "Hello, Dr. Sanchez."

The man nodded to him with a slight smile that wasn't at all infectious. He had the unrevealing eyes of a snake.

"It hardly matters if he knows you," Beed said to the man.

Dr. Sanchez said, "If it did, I wouldn't be here." He spoke with a slight accent, probably Cuban, and a calm authority that meant he was in charge. "Did you get what we want?"

"Haven't had a chance."

"What about next door?"

"Game old fucker," Beed said. "I worked on him last night until he lost consciousness once too often and I couldn't revive him. He never really spilled his guts, but whatever he knows, he won't be telling it around town."

"Val!" Hattie said. "What have you done to Val?"

"Old fart's in love with her," Beed said. "That's why he

wrote her those anonymous letters about her husband's death and got this whole mess started."

"*Val* wrote those letters?" Hattie said. So the culprit was right next door. She glanced over at Carver. What a detective he was.

Beed said, "Shut the fuck up." His professional veneer was falling away fast. He looked at Carver. "I followed you into Orlando and had a talk with Mark the friendly pharmacist, told him I was your assistant. He told me about that list of medications you showed him."

"Then I suppose Nurse Gorham checked the medical center files."

Nurse Gorham said, "I found a spreadsheet program in the files instead of the Keller Pharmaceutical disk, and the computerized Christmas card mailing list instead of Jerome Evans's medical history."

"How did you find out Val wrote the murder notes?" Carver asked.

Beed gave his narrow, bean-counter smile. "Afraid I'm a better detective than you are? That's one thing he told me under the influence of physical persuasion."

"You tortured him," Hattie said. "Your euphemisms won't alter that fact." She moved abruptly toward the door.

Beed grabbed her and she wheeled and tried to rake her fingernails across his eyes. He laughed and shoved her into the wall. Carver heard her head hit hard against it and she slid to the floor. He started to raise his cane to strike at Beed but the automatic's barrel swung his way.

Dr. Sanchez gripped Carver's arm, not so much to restrain him as to get him to change his mind about tangling with Beed. Hattie was lying on her back with her eyes closed. Carver was relieved to see her chest moving. She was breathing.

"She might be seriously hurt," he said.

Nurse Gorham's expression was bland as she walked over to Hattie and knelt beside her. She felt the pulse in her neck, lifted her eyelids and peered at her pupils, swiveled her head to examine where it had smacked the wall.

"She'll be okay," Nurse Gorham said in a professional tone. "Possible concussion, but that's about all." She smiled then and pinched Hattie's cheek.

"Monica likes to see people hurt sometimes," Beed said. "Gives her a tingle."

"That's the rumor," Carver said.

Nurse Gorham ignored them. "When the old lady regains consciousness, she needs to be watched."

"I hardly think so," Beed said.

Nurse Gorham and Dr. Sanchez looked at each other, then at Carver. The doctor said, "Save us the bother of searching the house for Jerome Evans's medication bottle, Mr. Carver. Save yourself a lot of bother."

"You're the only ones talking about a bottle," Carver said.

"No," Beed said, "before he, uh, lost the ability to converse, Val next door informed me that Hattie told him all about searching for the bottle. Your motel was being watched this morning. We figure you charged over here because Hattie called and said she'd found it. That means the bottle is here in the house, and you know where."

"Why's this bottle so important?" Carver asked.

"You know why, Mr. Carver," Dr. Sanchez said.

"Hattie told me she poured what was left of her husband's insomnia medication down the drain."

"I don't believe you, Mr. Carver. Neither do my associates."

"What's Luridus-X?" Carver asked.

"An experimental drug," Dr. Sanchez said.

"Why tell him?" Nurse Gorham asked.

"Why not?" Beed said, smiling at Carver. He sure had a

creepy smile, like a bookkeeper with secret hideous knowledge. Charles Manson's accountant.

"He's puzzled it out anyway," the doctor said. "That's why he's here." He clasped his narrow, feminine hands where his suit coat gaped in front and faced Carver squarely, a smugly confident man but with the human impulse to boast. "Mercury Laboratories is in the business of developing new and wonderful drugs, Mr. Carver. For this to be done with maximum effectiveness, tests have to be conducted. Solartown patients make ideal subjects. Sometimes the drugs are dispensed through the medical center pharmacy. Nurse Gorham administers the drugs secretly at the hospital, then monitors and reports results to Mercury."

"You might thank us someday if you become gravely ill," Nurse Gorham said.

Beed said, "Might not." He seemed amused that she couldn't shake her healer's instinct, even if she was a practicing sadist.

"Solartown residents provide perfect demographics for such experimentation," Dr. Sanchez continued. "The test subjects are all in the same age group, from the same general socioeconomic background, receive all their medical treatment at the center, and are easily available for tracking. And when the tests do occasionally go awry, a subject's death attracts little attention in a retirement community where advanced age makes death a frequent occurrence."

Carver had to admire such tidy logic and its implementation; Solartown patients were like custom-bred laboratory rats, only better. "Difficult to believe it all goes on under Dr. Wynn's nose," he said. It bothered him that Sanchez was talking so freely; it underlined that they fully intended to leave dead bodies in the house when they'd recovered the bottle. But he couldn't resist asking questions, now that he could get answers.

"Dr. Wynn has long had a serious addiction," Dr. Sanchez said.

"Drugs?"

"Me," Nurse Gorham said.

Dr. Sanchez raised a hand to silence her and continued talking, calmly and in an amiable tone, as if discussing a perfectly legal and respectable enterprise. "One night after an arranged evening of drinking with Nurse Gorham and Mr. Beed, Dr. Wynn was in an inebriated state and was indiscreet. His sexual adventures with both Mr. Beed and Nurse Gorham were videotaped."

"So he knows what's going on and you're blackmailing him into cooperation and silence."

"Paying him, actually," Dr. Sanchez corrected. "Still, Dr. Wynn understands the situation. When a Solartown test subject dies, he performs the autopsy, Nurse Gorham assisting, and signs the death certificate."

"But Dr. Billingsly's sure Jerome Evans died of a heart attack."

"And so he did. Evans was the test subject for a cholesterol-dissolving drug, placed in his sedative, that unfortunately didn't work out and produced massive blood clotting. So observation and the autopsy would reveal the cause of death to be an ordinary heart attack. Mercury has ceased researching and developing the drug."

"And now we want what's left of it back," Adam Beed said.

Dr. Sanchez fixed his unwavering cold gaze on Carver. "The residue in Jerome Evans's prescription bottle is evidence of what Florida law would consider homicide."

"The law and Jerome Evans—if he could speak from the grave."

"Not if he were a visionary, Mr. Carver. He'd understand that what we're doing here in Solartown is proper, that the overall benefits far outweigh the discomfort or even deaths of a few test subjects. They don't know it, but their last years of life are made into something beneficial and beautiful for mankind."

"Another thing they're doing is making Mercury Laboratories and its corporate officers wealthy."

Beed said, "Some black clouds have more than one silver lining."

Dr. Sanchez smiled with philosophical sadness. "Time for you to tell us where the bottle is, Mr. Carver."

"Can't do that," Carver said.

"I didn't think so." Dr. Sanchez turned his steady gaze on Beed.

Beed shoved the automatic's barrel hard into Carver's chest, causing him to stumble. Carver tried to catch himself with his cane but fell back into a sitting position in an upholstered chair with wooden arms. Beed aimed the automatic at his midsection and said, "Stay still; this won't hurt a bit."

Nurse Gorham drew a thick roll of broad white surgical tape from her purse and approached Carver. Quickly, deftly, she began taping his forearms to the chair arms, the calf and ankle of his good leg to a chair leg. The thigh of his stiff leg was taped against a chair-arm brace, and more tape was wrapped around his waist and the chair back.

When she was finished and Carver could barely move, she stepped back with obvious satisfaction and dropped what was left of the tape back in her purse.

"Shouldn't take long," Beed said.

"This should be fun to watch," Nurse Gorham said from deep in her throat. "Maybe fun to take part in."

Dr. Sanchez said, "I'd rather not watch, I'm in research. We'll be leaving. Call me when everything's settled, Adam."

"Mind waiting for a few minutes in the car?" Nurse Gorham asked. Her voice was tight, almost pleading.

"Come with me now, Monica," Dr. Sanchez said in an irritated tone. "This is business, not pleasure."

He and Nurse Gorham left by the front door. As she stepped out onto the porch, Nurse Gorham glanced back and smiled at Carver very much as Adam Beed was smiling.

|37|

BEED WALKED casually into the kitchen, and Carver heard water running. Splashing into something metallic.

A few minutes later Beed returned carrying several folded dish towels and a roasting pan half full of water. Some of the water sloshed onto the floor.

He scooted the chair over so it was facing away from the sofa, then tilted it back into the cushions so Carver was half reclining, staring up at the ceiling.

"In a little while you'll be dying to tell me everything from childhood on," Beed said. He began wrapping the towels around Carver's head and face, over his eyes, nose, and mouth. Carver could breathe, but it wasn't easy. As his vision was completely blocked, he had to resist the impulse to panic and squirm in the chair.

He was familiar with this method of torture and knew what was coming next. He told himself Beed was an expert and wouldn't let him drown. Not quite.

On the other hand, Beed was a fireball alcoholic no doubt twitching with his thirst, dangerous and unpredictable.

Water hit the towels, splashing coldly down Carver's chest and into his lap. Within seconds he felt the same chill on his face as the towels absorbed the water. Faintly he could hear Beed walking back and forth between the chair and the kitchen, refilling the blue metal pan and maybe other containers with water.

Every few minutes a torrent of water would hit Carver's head swaddled in the increasingly soaked towels. Water was in his mouth now, choking him as he tried to breathe.

He panicked and fought the tape binding him to the chair, hearing his own gurgling and retching cries muffled by the thick towels. Every heartbeat felt like a hot wire piercing his chest. Warmth suffused his drenched pants around his crotch; his bladder had released.

Then air and light, as the towels were unwound.

Beed was grinning down at him as if they were sharing a fun game. "Wanna do that again?"

Carver said nothing. He felt a stab of terror and something else as he saw that Beed was holding the half-full quart bourbon bottle from the kitchen.

Beed shrugged and wrapped the towels around Carver's head again, over his face.

More water.

Carver tried to hold his breath, but eventually exhaled rasping into the towels. His following inhalation brought water with it; he could actually feel its cold liquidity in his lungs as he gagged and tried to cry out. This was how it felt to breathe something other than air—he was drowning sitting in a chair!

Somehow he gained control and sat trembling. He could hear Beed make another trip to the kitchen to carry more water.

Beed let him wait in silence.

Minutes seemed to pass. Five of them, maybe ten.

Then more water splashed onto the towels.

A few seconds later, more water.

This wasn't going to happen with regularity; it would be impossible to predict and prepare for it.

Carver arched his back against his bonds but the tape didn't give. The effort made him inhale liquid and he coughed and gagged. He tried to plead, knowing Beed wouldn't understand him through the layers of wet towels.

No response. The towels remained. Carver managed to swallow enough water to allow himself to breathe. He waited in fear for another dousing and near drowning. Beed was boozing heavily on Hattie's liquor, he knew, losing life-saving judgment.

The waiting became almost as unbearable as the drowning sensation. Carver knew that was the way it was supposed to be, but it was impossible for him to make it any other way. Terror sapped logic and willpower; his responses were automatic and shamed and frightened him. That was how torture worked.

An immeasurable amount of time passed, perhaps even an hour, before the towels were again removed.

"Shall we chat now?" Beed asked, as Carver pulled in sweet, dry air and squinted into the light. Beed took a swig from the bottle and set it on the coffee table. It was only about a quarter full now. Beed didn't seem sober, didn't seem drunk.

But then an alky like Beed might be much drunker than he appeared.

Carver simply stared at him, trying not to rasp as he breathed.

Beed licked his lips, and something deep in his eyes changed, as if booze had overtaken reason and patience. He lost it then, said, "Fuck this!" He grabbed Carver's shirt and yanked Carver and the chair upright off the sofa cushions.

"Tell me where the bottle is!" Beed said, and backhanded Carver across the face.

Carver tried to roll with the blow but pain bit into him. Next came a punch to the stomach and his breath left him in a hollow scream. He would have doubled over, but that was impossible.

"You're making noise now, anyway," Beed said. "Ready to have that chat?"

Carver couldn't have answered if he'd tried. He tasted blood. Swallowed. Almost vomited.

Beed took another pull of bourbon, then swaggered into the kitchen.

Carver sat for a long time listening to things being banged around in there.

Beed wasn't carrying water when he returned this time. He had the length of black rubber hose from the spray attachment on the sink.

"This won't break any bones," he said, "but it'll bruise you clean through to the other side."

He began lashing back and forth through the air with the hose, then stepped forward so Carver was inside the dangerous arc.

Carver clenched his eyes shut. Pain hit him like successive lightning bolts as he writhed beneath the hose's dull and damaging repeated impacts.

"Start talking anytime," Beed said, working the hose with the effortless and relentless grace of a man scything weeds.

Carver glared at Beed, glanced at the bottle, and spat in Beed's face.

Beed stepped back in disbelief. Carver couldn't quite believe it himself. It had come from having nothing more to lose.

Beed shook for a few seconds with rage. Then he used his sleeve to wipe the spittle from his face, angled forward like a batter stepping up to the plate, and drew back the hose with both arms to lay it across Carver's head.

He stayed in that pose, like a TV freeze-frame, staring down at Carver with suspicion and puzzlement.

Then he dropped the hose and clutched his left arm, which

was pressed to his side. His mouth gaped wide as he struggled to speak. No sound came out. He looked like an old-time heavy overacting in a silent movie.

He staggered in a tight circle, drew a deep, screeching breath, then fell facedown on the carpet.

He didn't moan. He didn't move. He might as well have been furniture.

Carver sat trembling, sobbing with pain and trying to stay conscious.

38

HE WASN'T sure how much time had slipped past when he felt his bonds being cut away. He opened his eyes to see Beth standing over him, holding a long carving knife.

He tried to speak, but pain held the words inside him like a vise. He swallowed dryly. That hurt, too.

Beth sawed through some more tape binding his left arm to the chair and looked angry in a cold way Carver had seen only a few times.

"Hattie . . ." he finally heard himself mumble.

"She's okay, lover. Semiconscious, anyway." He could hear the blade severing tape from his arm, felt his partly numbed flesh pinched, maybe cut. Everything seemed to be happening at a distance.

"They had Val, too," he said, trying to pull himself into the here and now.

The blade ceased its sawing motion and Beth glanced around.

"He's next door," Carver told her.

"We'll take care of Val later."

When he was free, Beth handed him his cane and helped him to his feet. She was wearing a white summer dress this morning, high heels that made her slightly taller than Carver. "Gonna make it, Fred?"

He felt sore all over and there was fire along his rib cage. "Be okay if I keep moving and don't stiffen up," he said, already dreading tomorrow morning. He was sure to feel as if a bus had hit him then stopped and backed over him. "I wanna call Desoto, then let's get Hattie and Val to the medical center."

"Not to mention Fred," Beth said, and helped to support him as he limped over to the sofa and slumped in it with the phone in his lap. While he pecked out the number with a forefinger that had somehow become bruised and swollen, she went to tend to Hattie.

After he'd talked to Desoto, Carver found that some of the soreness had left him as his circulation returned where it had been constricted by the tape, which seemed to have gotten even tighter while wet. Other areas, especially his ribs and left shoulder, had become more tender. Man wasn't meant to be shrink-wrapped.

He and Beth managed to walk the semiconscious Hattie out to the rented Ford and get her settled in the backseat. Then they made their way up the driveway to Val's house.

After Carver used his cane to break one of the small windows in the door, and Beth snaked a long arm in and worked the deadbolt, they entered the house and found Val unconscious but still alive. He was bound to a chair as Carver had been, only with dozens of knotted neckties instead of tape. Shoots the hell out of his wardrobe, Carver thought inanely.

The fingertips of Val's right hand were bloody. He moaned and regained consciousness as Carver and Beth loosened the knots in the ties and worked his arms and legs free. Carver noticed a pair of pliers on the carpet, lying in the middle of dark stains and something else.

"Fingernails," Beth said levelly, seeing him staring.

Carver ground his teeth in rage, causing his jaw to flare in agony where he'd been struck.

Fingernails.

No wonder Val had talked.

Beth wrapped a towel from the bathroom around Val's mutilated hand, and Carver helped her walk him out to the Ford and get him in the back next to Hattie. He slumped low and closed his eyes, his bloody hand resting on his lap.

Beth looked at the frail, gray figures inside the car and said, "Hell of a way to treat senior citizens," still with the same icy anger.

"Or the middle-aged," Carver reminded her.

She stared at him with a tenderness in her eyes that somehow didn't touch the pinpoints of cold light in their centers.

"I'll drive," she said, and Carver handed her the keys.

On the way to the medical center Carver explained what had happened.

"Before Beed reached the house, I poured Jerome's medication into a bourbon bottle from one of the cabinets and left it on the counter. Then I tried to grind up the prescription bottle in the disposal and couldn't. But the bottle did jam the mechanism down out of sight in the plumbing. I knew if I simply tossed it into the trash or hid it and Beed found it, we'd all be useless to him and killed immediately."

"It figured an alky off the wagon would go for the booze," Beth said, staring straight ahead out the windshield, "but he mighta consumed all of exhibit A."

"He drank most of it," Carver said, "but there should still be enough left in the bottle that it can be separated from the bourbon and analyzed. Or they can analyze Beed's stomach contents. Either way, it'll make the case against Mercury Laboratories."

"So Beed went the same way Jerome Evans did," Beth said.

"Sudden massive coronary." She smiled in a way Carver didn't like. "Hattie'll appreciate that."

Carver thought she was probably right. These two women from different backgrounds might understand each other in a way he could never fathom. Beth had once told Carver he had a prehistoric view of women. Called him a dinosaur, specifically a brontosaurus, but said he could learn from her.

She tapped the horn as they pulled into the medical center driveway, then parked by the Emergency doors and ran inside.

Less than a minute later, several attendants and Solartown volunteers bustled out with stainless steel wheelchairs and removed Hattie and Val from the back of the Ford, rolled them into the medical center.

"This one, too," Beth said, pointing to Carver.

"Not yet," he told the young nurse who was appraising him while moving toward him. He pushed past her and limped in through the darkly tinted glass doors, Beth close behind him. The pain in his ribs was getting worse, making him take shallow breaths that hit like fresh blows from the rubber hose.

Emergency was tiled and painted in shades of green. There was a long counter with computers on it, a small waiting area lined with brown plastic chairs. Two old women sat in the end chairs near the TV jutting from the wall, staring not at the game show in progress but at what was going on around them. A dog-eared *Reader's Digest* slipped off the lap of one of them and dropped to the floor, but she didn't notice.

Several wide halls led from the admitting area, two of them sectioned off by swinging doors.

The old man Carver had seen drive into the Warm Sands lot after Roger Karl's body was found in Carver's car was leaning against the wall near the waiting area.

He strutted over to Carver and said, "I'm Commander Rubin, Solartown Posse. That Dr. Sanchez shagged ass outa here just after I picked up the call on the police frequency. Two Posse patrol units pulled his car over near the highway exit. Against the rules, but what the hell? He didn't resist. He's being held till the other police get there."

"Right now," Carver said, noticing that Rubin smelled strongly and dizzyingly of pipe tobacco, "what I'm interested in—"

He stopped talking as he saw Dr. Wynn and Nurse Gorham approaching. They were halfway down the long hall and hadn't noticed him. He moved over out of line with the doorway, almost out of sight, but where he still had a narrow view of the hall. Waited. Commander Rubin squinted at him and stepped aside, as if Carver might have been struck unaccountably mad and needed reassessment. But Beth had observed him and figured out what was happening.

Wynn saw Hattie Evans being wheeled into one of the observation rooms and stopped. Nurse Gorham, surprised, halted with him, so abruptly that her rubber-soled white shoes *eep*ed on the tile floor.

It was too late. They were already too far into the waiting room and couldn't retreat.

Wynn turned, saw Carver, and froze while realization and fear distorted his features. He instinctively started to bolt. Carver brought his cane across the doctor's back and he stumbled and fell. He scrambled to get up and run, making it halfway to his feet, but Carver tripped him with the crook of the cane and he fell again. This time he crawled to a corner and sat curled with his head bowed.

Nurse Gorham had stood paralyzed and watching during the few seconds this had taken. Then she moved. Maybe she'd recovered from shock and intended to run, or maybe she was simply walking over to stand by Wynn. She only managed two steps before one of Beth's black high heels flashed out and slammed into the back of her nyloned knee, driving her to the floor.

On her hands and knees, eyes wide with astonishment, she turned around awkwardly on the hard tiles and struggled to rise.

The shoe darted out again, catching her squarely in the side of the neck with a sound Carver felt in his stomach. Nurse Gorham lay flat on her back, whimpering in pain and pawing the air in slow motion with clawlike hands.

Beth, standing over her, said, "Guess you changed your mind about leaving." Carver knew she'd said it to plant in the minds of witnesses that Nurse Gorham had attempted to escape, and the violence had been necessary. Beth covering herself in the event of future litigation.

Carver stared, feeling his heart banging away at his sore ribs, and said, "Christ!"

Beth smiled over at him, then calmly and with accuracy spat on Nurse Gorham.

Said, "You need a wheelchair, Fred."

39

IT WAS a week before Carver's bruises began to fade. He'd suffered two hairline rib fractures on his left side, and he still wore elasticized wrapping around his midsection most of the time. The pain still sneaked up on him at night, or grabbed him after sudden movement, but less frequently now and with less bite.

He and Beth stayed at the Warm Sands while he healed, giving up her room so she could move in with him.

They were lying now on the artificial beach, side by side on large towels they'd carried down from the room. Carver was on his back with his eyes closed, letting the sun do its healing work, listening to the shouts and laughter of kids down by the artificial lake.

His eyelids fluttered as he felt Beth's light touch on his bare chest, the pleasant coolness of the suntan lotion she was rubbing into him with soft circular motions. She had hands like no woman he'd ever known.

"I got a call from Hattie this morning," she said.

Carver said, "Hmm."

"She's feeling pretty good now, comparatively. Jaw still hurts, but it's getting better. Least you can understand her on the phone okay."

Women and phones, Carver the brontosaurus thought.

"She didn't say it, but she's enjoying nursing Val back to health, taking care of him. She called from his house. I don't think she's spending much time in hers these days."

"Hmm."

"Things work out for people sometimes," Beth said, "if they just keep keepin' on. That old bastard Val's finally got what he wanted. He's happy as a pig in shit just to lie around and let Hattie nurse him. Kinda pathetic."

Carver didn't say anything. A warm breeze moved over his body. Beth's hands continued to work their miracle. He knew exactly how Val must feel. Felt the same way himself.

Liked it.

M
F
LUT   Spark

Lutz

COPY 1